# Lily's Ultimate Party

Young Women of Faith

# Lily's Ultimate Party

## Nancy Rue

Zonderkidz

Zonder**kidz**™

*The children's group of Zondervan*

*Lily's Ultimate Party*
Copyright © 2001 by Women of Faith

Requests for information should be addressed to:
Zonderkidz, *Grand Rapids, Michigan 49530*
www.zonderkidz.com

ISBN: 0-310-23253-8

Zonderkidz is a trademark of Zondervan.

Published in association with the literary agency of Alive Communications, Inc., 7680 Goddard Street, Suite 200, Colorado Springs, CO 80920.

*Art direction and interior design by Amy Langeler*

*Printed in the United States of America*

02 03 04 05 06/❖ DC/ 10 9 8 7 6 5 4

# Chapter 1

"Man, this is the lamest party on the planet."

Shad Shifferdecker's too-close-together eyes went right to Lily. She tossed her curly mane of red hair.

"Don't look at *me*," she said. "I didn't plan it."

Shad sauntered off toward the refreshment table to join his two buddies, Leo Cooks and Daniel Tibbetts, who were hovering suspiciously over the onion dip. For once Shad was right. Kids were standing around beneath the limp crepe-paper streamers looking more like they were at the bus stop than a sixth-grade graduation party. Lily looked around for her own friends.

She didn't have far to look. Her best friend, Reni Johnson, was hurrying toward her from the door, holding a piece of paper high over her braid-covered head, her dark eyes sparkling.

"Hey, Lil!" She flapped the piece of paper. "Look at this!"

"Look at what?" Shad said.

Before Reni could give the paper another flap, Shad was on her, his two sidekicks with him. Leo snatched it from her fingers and passed it off to Daniel. Reni made a lunge for it, but they got her between them in a human cage while Shad grabbed the paper from Daniel.

"Shad, that is so rude!" That, of course, came from Marcie McCleary, who was immediately on the scene as usual. She was in the middle of everything but the teachers' lounge. "You're always so rude," she said again, and then jumped up to try to get the paper herself.

Shad evaded her neatly and grinned like the Tasmanian Devil at the document in his hand. But the grin disappeared instantly, and he gave a disgusted hiss as he let it drop to the floor. Reni snatched it up before Marcie could dive for it.

"What'd it say, man?" Leo said, still straining to get a peek.

"Nothin'," Shad said. "*Dude,* this party is lame!"

"Cake, anyone?"

It was Ms. Gooch, sweeping into the multipurpose room carrying a sheet cake. Lily was sure it had something on it like, "Congratulations Graduates," in too-sweet frosting, right next to the Cedar Hills Elementary School logo of a demented-looking house cat that was supposed to look like a cougar.

Most of the graduates charged the table, but Lily turned to Reni, who was still blowing Shad germs off of her piece of paper.

"What is that, Ren?" Lily said. "Why wouldn't Shad read it?"

"'Cause he probably couldn't," Reni said, glaring in his direction.

"Yeah," said a voice behind them. It was Zooey Hoffman, another member of their Girlz Only Club. "He's the dumbest boy in the whole *universe.*" Her blue eyes got bigger in her round face. "You know that part in the graduation when we were supposed to shake hands with everybody around us?"

By now their friends Suzy Wheeler and Kresha Ragina had joined them. Zooey's eyes bulged bigger still, and the ponytail secured by a scrunchie on top of her head wiggled.

"Just before he stuck out his hand to me, he *spit* in it!"

"Gross!" they cried in unison.

Suzy shuddered. "Did you actually—touch it?"

Zooey nodded solemnly and produced her hand for them to inspect.

"So what's on that paper?" Lily asked Reni.

Reni broke back into a grin. "I got recommended for orchestra at the middle school!"

"Vhat is 'orchestra'?" Kresha said. She was from Croatia. A lot of things in English got by her.

"You remember when we got to try all kinds of instruments in music?" Suzy explained patiently.

"All of us stunk at it," Lily said. "Except you, Reni."

Reni was looking taller than her usual elflike self. "I get to be in orchestra! It's a really big deal at Middle. You get to wear a long dress and miss school to play at luncheons and stuff."

"This is cool, Ren," Lily said.

"It totally is. I'm so jazzed—" Reni stopped, and her eyes drooped a little. "The only thing is—you won't be in it with me."

Lily shook her head. "We'll still hang out all the time," she said. "You aren't gonna be playing the violin every *minute*."

"I know," Reni said. "But we've always done everything together and—well, are you sure you don't feel left out?"

"Nah," Lily said. "We already have one musician in our family. That's Art's thing."

"Whew," Reni said. "I was afraid it was gonna be funky."

"Nah," Lily said. "No way."

That was absolutely the truth. But as Lily followed Reni to the table for a piece of cougar cake, she did feel an old, familiar, nagging tug at her. It was more like words in her head than a feeling. They said, *So, what is your thing, Lily? Mom and Joe are athletes. Dad's this smart person who writes. Art plays the saxophone like a mad dog. What are you known for?*

Lily absently took the paper plate with cake that Ms. Gooch handed her. She'd already tried modeling, medicine, and women's libbing, and although she'd learned something about all of them, they'd turned out not to be who she was.

She stabbed at the tip of the cougar's frosted tail with the plastic fork. *When am I gonna find out why I'm here?* she thought.

"You don't have to kill it, Robbins," someone said at her elbow.

Lily didn't have to look up to know it was Ashley Adamson. Ashley had started calling everyone by last names, and so, of course, had most of the other girls in the class—Chelsea Green and Marcie—well, everybody but the Girlz Only Club.

"Why did you chop up your cake like that, Robbins?" Ashley said.

Lily looked at the mess of crumb clumps on the Graduation Day paper plate and felt her face go blotchy in that way her brother Joe always said made her look like she had a disease. But to her surprise, Ashley leaned her head in a little closer and whispered, "It *does* taste pretty nasty. This is, like, the worst party."

"Yeah," Lily said.

Ashley jerked an eyebrow toward the ceiling. "Stupid decorations. Disgusting food. Elevator music. Nothing to do."

"All right, middle schoolers!" Ms. Gooch sang out just then. "How about one last class activity?"

The room filled with one big moan.

"This is gonna be dumb," Ashley muttered. "Why did I open my mouth? It was better when we were just standing around."

"I hear ya," Lily said.

Suddenly, Ashley looked startled, as if she just realized she was having a conversation with a nonfriend. But as she scurried away calling "McCleary? Green?" Lily wasn't disappointed. She was too busy meeting up with a new idea—an idea that could set her apart from every person in the room.

She announced it to her mom in the kitchen the next morning while Mom was cleaning out the refrigerator.

"I want to have a party," Lily said.

"As long as it isn't in the next twenty-four hours, fine," Mom said. She opened a Tupperware container, sniffed at it, and crossed her brown doe eyes. "It's going to take me that long to get to the back of this refrigerator."

"I don't get why you're doing that now," Lily's sixteen-year-old brother Art said as he strolled into the kitchen and began prowling in the food cabinet. "I thought we were going to Mudda's this weekend."

"We are," Mom said. "But I have exactly one week off before volleyball camp starts, and if I don't clean this out, we're going to be able to manufacture penicillin in here. What is *this*?"

Art looked over her shoulder at the plastic container she was peering into. "I think at one time it was lemon slices," he said. "Now it's maggot food."

"Cool!" That came from nine-year-old Joe, who tossed his baseball glove on the table, missing Lily's arm by a hair's width. "Let me see!"

"All lookers have to help," Mom said.

Joe did an about-face and followed Art back to the food cabinet, where they both proceeded to forage.

Lily took a big breath to help her sound patient, something it was always hard to do when her brothers were around. "I'll help, Mom," she said, "but can we talk about my party while we're doing this?"

"What party?" Joe said.

"You aren't invited," Lily said. "So, Mom, could we?"

"Get me a big garbage bag, would you?" Mom said.

Lily stifled a loud sigh as she pulled one out from under the sink and held it open while Mom dumped unrecognizable objects into it. Munching on Pop Tarts, Joe and Art settled themselves at the table.

"Let me know if you find anything with bugs in it," Joe said.

"You'll be the first to know," Mom said dryly.

"So—the party," Lily said.

"Sure," Mom said. "When we get back from Mudda's—then, whatever."

"What I wanna know," Joe said, "is do I still have to call her Mudda?"

"Ask your brother," Mom said. "He's the one who named her that."

"I couldn't say 'Grandmother' when I was a baby, okay?" Art said. "I didn't know it was gonna haunt me for the rest of my life."

"Call her whatever you want," Mom said. But then she pulled her head out of the vegetable crisper and added, "Nothing disrespectful."

"Sorry, bro," Art said to Joe. "I guess 'Hey, old lady' is out of the question."

"Art," Mom said in her warning tone. She seldom got stern. She didn't have to. All three of them had learned what that warning tone meant: push it any further, and you're dog meat.

"I know your grandmother isn't the easiest person to get along with," Mom continued, tossing a piece of lettuce out of her brown-sugar-colored ponytail, "but your father and I still expect you to be decent to her."

"So, can I follow you guys in Ruby Sue?" Art asked.

That was his name for the old Subaru he drove. Ever since he'd gotten his license a month before, he wanted to drive everywhere.

"No—you can ride in the van with us," Mom said. She produced a plastic bag with something slimy in it. "Lil, what do you suppose that is?"

"If you can't identify it, Mom, I suggest you throw it out," Art said. "While you're in there, is there any butter—I mean that's edible?"

Mom shot him a look, and Art ate his Pop Tart butterless.

"So, I want to start planning my party," Lily said.

"What's to plan?" Mom asked. "You invite the girls over, I pick up some snacks from Sam's Club, and you sleep all over the family room."

"It isn't going to be that kind of party," Lily said. "I want it to be way cooler than anything anybody in my class ever gave—definitely better than that lame thing they threw for us last night."

"I remember my sixth-grade graduation gig," Art said. He tilted his chair back on two legs and looked off into the distance with his eyes like Mom's, scratching his short curly hair as if he were recalling some event from a previous decade. "Sawdust cake. Bad music. Duck-duck-goose."

"Duck-duck-goose?" Joe said. "We don't even play that in third grade! Dude!"

"Right," Lily cut in while Joe was guffawing himself up to Art's level. "I don't want a party like that. I want *the* coolest party—and I want to have boys too."

There was a silence so solid in the kitchen that Lily wished she'd thought of mentioning boys before if it quieted everybody down that fast. Art stopped with the Pop Tart midway to his mouth, and Joe could only blink as if he were in shock. Mom was the first to break the silence and say, "Don't you have enough maleness around here?"

"Nobody's had a boy-girl party yet," Lily said. "I want to be the first."

Mom looked thoughtfully at the expiration date on a tub of yogurt. "It's not like I'm not used to boys cluttering up the place," she said.

"Did she just call us clutter?" Joe said to Art.

"Yeah, she did," Art said.

"So I don't see why not," Mom said. "But can you wait until we get back from Mudda's Monday?"

"Oh, yikes, yes!" Lily said. "This is gonna take me at least a month to plan and get ready."

The corners of Mom's mouth were twitching. Mom didn't smile that much, but Lily knew the corner thing. It meant she found whatever Lily was saying pretty amusing.

"I bet it takes a lot to make a party perfect," Lily said.

"I certainly wouldn't know." There was more twitching. "But I do know you're going to find out everything there is *to* know and then some."

"Aw, man," Art groaned. "I hate it when she gets all into something. She's gonna turn into Martha Stewart!"

Lily ignored him. The wheels were already turning in her head. Straight to the library for a book on parties. Then a trip to the Parties-R-Us store for ideas. And they were bound to have stuff about entertaining on the Home and Garden channel—if she could ever get the remote away from Joe and Art. But Art was doing band camp all summer, and Joe would be going from Little League games to soccer practice to whatever other ball-related thing he could squeeze in. It would just be her, quietly idea gathering.

With the Girlz, of course. Nothing was that much fun without her Girlz. She went to the phone to call a meeting.

Chapter
2

But the phone calls to the Girlz weren't what Lily hoped for. Suzy was going shopping with her mother for new clothes and shoes. She was starting soccer camp Monday—a special by-invitation-only camp she had been doing handsprings about since April.

"I'm sorry, Lily," she said on the phone. "I really want to be with you guys, but I have to have the right stuff for this camp."

"No problem," Lily said. "We'll remember everything and tell you all about it. But I hope you don't have a game or something the night of my party."

Lily paused, waiting for Suzy to promise that she would miss a World Cup play-off for Lily's shindig, but Suzy paused even longer. Lily could imagine her fiddling with a piece of her shiny black hair. Finally, she said, "How about if I give you my schedule when I get it?"

"Oh," Lily said. "Okay."

But it still didn't bother her too much—until she made the next phone call.

"Ren," she said, "we gotta have a meeting today."

"I can't today," Reni said. "Guess what?"

"What?"

"I get to take private violin lessons! My dad was so impressed I got into orchestra he took me out this morning and rented me an instrument, and this afternoon we're gonna go interview two teachers."

"That's cool!" Lily said. But she was starting to wilt. "So—when *will* you be free?"

"I don't know. I don't know when my lessons are gonna be or how much I'm gonna have to practice. But I wanna be the *best* when school starts. I still can't believe I got picked!"

Lily felt limp when she hung up.

Then she called Kresha. But Kresha was with her English-as-a-second-language tutor.

She called Zooey. Finally, somebody was excited for *her*.

"You get to give a boy-girl party?" Zooey said. "Lucky. My mom would never let me—not in a thousand million years."

"That's okay," Lily said, spirits perking up a little. "You can help me with mine. You want to get together today?"

Zooey sighed into the phone. Zooey did a lot of sighing.

"I can't," she said. "My mom's making me take swimming lessons."

"Oh," Lily said. Good grief! Even Zooey had more of a life than she did.

"But she also said she'd take me to buy a new swimsuit," Zooey was saying. "So I guess it's okay. What about tomorrow?"

"I'm leaving for my grandmother's tomorrow," Lily said. "I'll call you Monday when I get back."

But when she hung up, Lily felt deflated. Was Monday going to be any better with Reni taking violin lessons and Suzy going to soccer camp and Zooey learning to swim and Kresha practicing her English? Suddenly, it seemed more important than ever to focus on the party planning. She went on a hunt in Dad's study for a pad to write on.

By the time the Robbins family got to Carlisle, Pennsylvania, the next afternoon, Lily had the pad half filled. One whole page was the guest list (it was up to thirty people). It took three pages for the food list. To include all the stuff she and the Girlz liked, she was going to have to serve everything from stuffed mushrooms to corn dogs—and then there were boys' appetites to consider. If the guys in her class ate the way Art and Joe did, that was going to mean huge piles of nachos and probably several extra-large pizzas with everything but anchovies.

She was on her tenth page of decoration ideas when they pulled up to Mudda's house. Mudda was waiting for them on the front steps. Her short, crisply cut hair was shining like a silver helmet.

"What took you so long?" she scolded as she deposited a kiss on Dad's cheek. "I've been waiting for you since seven."

"Hi, Mom," Dad said. "Nice to see you too."

His blue eyes twinkled behind his glasses. Art's and Joe's rolled as they took their turns getting kissed and inspected.

"Arthur, you've grown a foot," Mudda said. "When are *you* going to start sprouting up, Joseph? It's too much junk food is what it is."

"It's hopeless, Mudda," Mom said. "He's a junkie. We've tried rehab—locking him in the closet—nothing works."

The corners of her mouth twitched as she gave Mudda a squeeze. Lily's grandmother scowled, drawing her wide-like-Lily's mouth into a bunch and narrowing her bright-blue eyes until the wrinkles spread out like cobwebs on her temples.

"It's nothing to joke around about, Joanna," she said to Mom. "The boy needs his vitamins."

"I get plenty of vitamins," Joe said. "You should see all the broccoli she makes me eat. Did you make any snickerdoodles?"

"Yes, but there will be none of that until you have lunch. Well, Lilianna, are you going to say hello or ignore me?"

Lily shifted the pad to her left hand and hugged Mudda's neck with her right. Her grandmother planted a dry kiss on her cheek and then pulled back to survey her through the bottom halves of her glasses as if she were checking her for something microscopic.

"You still have the Robbins clear skin," she said. "I don't see any pimples yet."

"You just can't see them for the freckles," Joe said.

He and Art high-fived each other, and Lily glared at them both.

"Well, for heaven sake, come on in out of the heat," Mudda said. "I've got lunch ready—if it isn't ruined."

"On my best day I couldn't fix a lunch as delicious as one of your 'ruined' ones," Mom said.

As they stepped into the house, Mudda began the usual litany of things that had to be done while they were there. Lily saw Mom clap a hand over Joe's mouth so nobody could hear him moaning.

"There's a whole box of books up in the attic I want you to go through, all of you, and take home what you want. The rest are going to the rummage sale. I'm starting to clear things out around here."

"Mom, you've been saying that ever since Dad died," Lily's father said.

"You kids never stay long enough to do any sorting," she said. "What do I get you for this time—twenty-four hours?"

"Oh, no," Art said. "It's three whole days, Mudda." He said it as if it might as well have been forever.

Mom shot him a warning look and ushered them to the table.

"You never eat half of what I fix," Mudda said.

"Then maybe you oughta only fix half as much," Joe said.

Everybody else in the Robbins family said, "Joe!"

"He's got a fresh mouth on him, Paul," Mudda said to Dad.

"I should leave him here with you for a week," Mom said, mouth twitching. "That would straighten him out."

Lily thought Joe was going to go into convulsions.

Everybody stuffed as many ham sandwiches and as much potato salad into themselves as Mudda required before she would bring out the snickerdoodles. By then the conversation had turned to what every single one of Dad's other relatives was doing, saying, and being treated by a doctor for, and even snickerdoodles weren't enough to keep the kids at the table.

"Did you get cable yet?" Joe said when Mudda took a breath.

"You're not just going to plug yourself in at my house," Mudda said.

"Why don't you guys all start with that box in the attic," Mom said quickly. "When you've done that, then you can watch some TV."

Taking a snickerdoodle each for the trek up to the third floor, they exited the kitchen to the sound of Mudda explaining the evils of too much television to Mom and Dad.

The air got hotter and stuffier as Joe and Art took the last flight of stairs, and they were already wiping off sweat and complaining. Lily scooped her tangle of curls into a ponytail with the scrunchie she kept on her wrist for just such occasions.

"Has Mudda always been that cranky?" Art said as he opened the door to the oven of an attic.

"Yes," Joe said.

But Lily shook her head at Art. "When you and I were really little, she wasn't so bad. Mom says she's just getting older and that makes her grouchy."

"Grouchy?" Joe said. "She's a witch!"

"Yeah, well, don't say it in front of her or Mom's liable to make you stay here," Art said.

"No way!" Joe said.

Lily looked around for the box of books. She'd figured out a long time ago that if you did what Mudda said, she stayed pretty much off your case.

As she scoped out the attic, Lily saw that there were a whole bunch of boxes up there, and the first three she opened were full of papers yellowed at the edges. The fourth one had magazines in it, and Lily was about to close it up too when something on the cover of the one on top caught her eye.

*Throw the Ultimate Backyard Party This Summer,* it read.

Lily pulled the magazine out of the box and flipped through its dusty pages. She knew the article the minute she came to it—there was a two-page picture spread that jumped right out at her.

Pictures of bright invitations that looked like beach towels . . . photographs of tables piled with watermelon shells full of tropical fruit and salads shaped like sea turtles . . . photos of seashell sculptures and sparkling papier-mâché sand castles decorating somebody's whole patio. Lily felt her face splitting into a grin.

"What's the matter with you, Lily?" Joe said. "Did that potato salad give you gas?"

Art took the magazine out of her hand.

"Tell me this isn't what you're gonna try to pull off in our backyard," he said, thumping the party pictures with his finger.

Lily followed it to the page, and the most brilliant of ideas took instant shape in her mind. Until that very moment, she hadn't known what the magazine meant, but now that Art mentioned it—well, what could be more perfect?

By now Joe was craning his neck to see around Art's elbow. "Why is the kiddie pool full of sodas?" he said.

"It is?" Lily said. She pulled the magazine away from Art. There *was* a kids' pool—filled with ice and pop cans—and there was a beach umbrella keeping it all in the shade.

"Dude, she's got that I'm-about-to-go-ballistic-over-this look," Art said.

Lily ignored him. She was already mentally tossing out the party pad and starting over—with the Ultimate Backyard Party.

Joe and Art had already glanced through the finally discovered box of books and decided there was nothing worth reading in it and were down in the television room flipping channels when Lily heard a throat being cleared in the doorway. She looked up to see Mudda's eyes narrowed tightly.

Lily flashed her a smile. "I didn't want any of the books either," she said. "But I found a good magazine."

Mudda put her hand out, and Lily scrambled up off the floor and placed the June 1970 *Family Circle* magazine in it.

"What do you want with this?" Mudda said.

"I'm having a party this summer, and I want it to be just like the one in the pictures. It's kind of old-fashioned, so it won't be like any party anybody else would think of."

Mudda shifted her slitted eyes from the magazine to Lily's face. "Is that why you're giving the party, Lilianna?" she said. "To impress everyone?"

"Well, yeah—" Lily said. She blinked at her grandmother. "I mean it isn't, like, the *only* reason—"

"Heavens, child, you're starting to sound like a silly teenager. 'Yeah' and 'like.' I always thought you'd stay away from slang. Your father did, you know."

Lily said she was sorry because she didn't know what else to say.

"You've always been a good student," Mudda went on. "Not as exceptional as your father, but then, he's brilliant, and brilliance doesn't come along that often."

"I know," Lily said. She'd never been the target of Mudda's stinging tongue before, and for once her own tongue was tied in a knot.

"Still, I hoped you wouldn't start acting ridiculous when you got ready to start middle school."

"Oh!" Lily said. She felt a little wobbly with relief. "I'm not going to act ridiculous, Mudda! I can't stand girls who are ridiculous."

"I'm not talking about other girls. Other girls don't carry the name Lily Robbins, and you do. I gave it a good reputation, and I should think you'd want to do the same."

Lily had to take a few seconds to untangle that one. Her grandmother's name was Lilian, so Lily had been named after her, although her mom had added the *na* on the end of her name so she'd have her own identity. It sounded like Mudda was forgetting the *na* altogether.

"Don't worry," Lily said. "I'll keep the name good."

Her grandmother closed her eyes completely. "You won't do it with grammar like that," she said. "Give me a week with you, and I'd have that cleaned up."

Lily froze. *Stay with you for a week?* she wanted to wail. *I'll totally die!* For once, she knew exactly how Joe felt.

"You know what it means to be Lily Robbins, don't you?"

Lily snapped back to her. "Huh?" she said.

"How can you have such a marvelously articulate father and blurt out something like 'huh'?"

"I meant to say 'excuse me,'" Lily said lamely. "That just sort of popped out. It's from being in the car with Joe and Art all day."

"If they had that much influence on your behavior, you would currently be sitting in front of the television making repulsive noises with your armpit." Mudda shook her head. "You're responsible for yourself, Lilianna. I'm going to keep reminding you of that."

Lily felt as if her stomach were sinking. Mudda didn't say she was going to do something and then not carry it out all the way. This could turn into a very long weekend.

And it was. At the dinner table, when Lily said she didn't care for any coleslaw with her crab cakes, Mudda said she was trying to be a skeleton like every other ridiculous young woman in America.

Before bed, when Lily put on one of Dad's university T-shirts to sleep in, Mudda said she was trying to act like a coed and that she ought to be wearing cute little pajamas.

The next day, when Lily was dutifully pawing through junk in the garage, Mudda told her she'd developed a bad habit of slouching when she ought to be proud of her height.

Lily tried retreating to the room she was staying in on the second floor and studying the ultimate party article in the *Family Circle*. But about the time she finally got absorbed, she heard Mudda on the stairs, talking to Mom and Dad.

"You give me a week with her," Mudda was saying.

"I don't know," Lily's mother said. "She's the only other person in the house who doesn't leave the toilet seat up."

*No, Mom!* Lily wanted to scream. *You're making it worse!*

"I'd love for Lilliputian to spend a week with you, Mom," Dad said.

Lily gripped the bedspread so hard her knuckles lost their color.

"But are you sure you're up for it?" he went on. "You look tired to me."

"I'm sixty-one years old. Of course I look tired. But that doesn't mean I can't handle a twelve-year-old girl."

"The question is, can she handle you?" Mom said.

"Don't be ridiculous. What is there to 'handle'?"

*Being told how horrible I am every second!* By now Lily was at the door, her ear pressed against the wood.

"I have an idea that I think will make everybody happy," Dad said. "I think Mom should come stay with us for a week. She could spend time with Lily when she wanted to and have a chance to rest too."

"Now, there's a thought—" Mom started to say.

But Mudda cut in. "I'm not going to go to all the trouble to close up this house just to go away for a week. If I'm going to come, it's going to be for at least a month."

"Of course, Mom!" Dad said. "You're welcome to stay as long as you want!"

Lily sagged against the door and watched her wonderful party summer slip away.

Chapter 3

On the way home Monday night, all Lily could do was stare out the van window and envision what it was going to be like having Mudda in the house—and in Lily's face—for a whole month.

Lily was so bummed out that she barely smiled when they stopped at Friendly's for supper and ice-cream sundaes.

"All right, what's the deal, Lil?" Mom said when they were in the restroom together.

Lily turned on the hand dryer so she could pretend she didn't hear her, but Mom was patient. She *always* had all the time in the world when Lily wanted to avoid an issue.

"I don't know," Lily lied when Mom outwaited her at the sink.

"I think I do," Mom said. "I think you need something to occupy you this summer."

"I have my party to plan," Lily said faintly, although right now, even that didn't sound like enough to compete with her grandmother's plan to give Lily a personality transplant.

"Yeah, well, I'm talking about something a little more structured," Mom said. "There aren't any classes you want to take?"

Lily shook her head.

"That's a first." Mom twisted her lips the way she did when she was thinking hard. "When we get home, let's look for something you can do at home on your own. I get a little nervous when you have too much free time on your hands."

Lily felt her face and neck going blotchy. "Why is it that everybody all of a sudden thinks I'm some slob or something?"

"Whoa, girlfriend. I didn't say you were a slob." Mom touched the tip of Lily's nose. "I just like to stay ahead of that imagination of yours, that's all."

*Yeah,* Lily thought. *And Mudda wants to wipe it out completely.*

But she didn't say anything. At least she'd gotten out of Mudda's house with the *Family Circle* magazine.

When they got home, even after Mom took her to the Christian bookstore the next day and bought her a Bible study course for girls, complete with journal and cool pens, Lily set up her own structure. After all, there was still a week before Mudda was due to arrive. If she at least had the party all set to roll by then, her grandmother would see that Lily was too much her own person to change.

So every morning before the boys even rolled out for baseball practice and band camp, Lily was parked in front of the Home and Garden channel with a bowl of Cheerios and her pen, waiting for party tips.

When everybody else got up, she retreated to her room, did her Bible study for the day at lightning speed, and then combed the Old Testament for examples of festivals and banquets, so that when Mom came in she always had the NIV open and her pen poised.

She did like the journal that came with the Bible study course. It gave her a private place to record her progress with the party. By Thursday evening, she had a plan to show Mom and Dad. She called Reni just before going down to the family room to present it. Reni was always good for a pep talk—when she was home.

Every time Lily had called her since she'd been back from Mudda's, Reni had either been at a lesson or involved in a practice session. Lily was relieved tonight that she didn't hear the screeching of violin strings in the background when Reni's mom answered.

"Hi!" Reni said when she got to the phone. "Guess what?"

"What?" Lily said. She tried not to sound like she couldn't wait to talk about *her* stuff.

"We found the coolest teacher! He's a professor at the college, but he gives private lessons in summer. His name's Sigmund, and he has all this wild hair—wilder than yours, even—and he's a virtuosity!"

Lily could hear Reni's mom's voice in the background, and Reni giggled. "I mean virtuoso," she said.

"Oh. Well, cool. Um, Reni, could you take the phone to someplace where we can, like, you know, talk privately?"

"Sure," Reni said. "So, anyway, I go to lessons twice a week because he says I have talent and I could make a lot of progress this summer if I practice at least an hour a day, only I'm practicing two because I don't just want to be good—I want to be great. Okay, I'm in my room. What's going on?"

Lily spilled everything—all about Mudda and the personality transplant and the hurt feelings and the ordeal of having her in the house forever. Most of all, though, she told her about the party.

"So you gotta help me," Lily said when she was nearly finished. "I want this to be the ultimate party. That's what the magazine says—ultimate. I know we don't have a built-in pool, but our above-ground one is pretty cool, I mean, it's got the deck and everything."

"There's no way I'm not helping you with this party," Reni said. "When's it gonna be?"

"July 15th," Lily said. She was feeling happier already.

"I can't do it that day. I have a lesson."

"Oh," Lily said. "Can't you change it?"

"Are you kidding?" Reni said. "I was lucky to even get in with Sigmund. If I start changing things around so I can go to a party, he'll think I'm not serious. And I am *so* serious."

"So am I," Lily said.

"Can't *you* pick another day?" Reni said. "Or did you already send out the invitations?"

That showed what Reni knew about giving parties. The magazine said the invitations shouldn't be sent out more than two weeks ahead of time. It was plain Lily was going to have to educate the Girlz about the art of entertaining—*if* she could ever get them all together.

After she and Reni agreed that the sixteenth would be a better day, she called Suzy to check with her. She had a soccer tournament that whole weekend. Lily moved the party date to the twenty-third, which was even better, because by then Mudda would be gone.

A quick call back to Reni confirmed that the twenty-third was fine with her, as long as it was after noon. Kresha was okay with that too. Except for English lessons, Kresha had no life either. Lily was sure it would be fine with Zooey as well.

And it was—until Lily mentioned that it was going to be a back-yard beach party and they were all going to swim in the Robbins' pool. There was a long, heavy pause on the other end of the phone line.

"You still there, Zooey?" Lily said.

"Yeah," Zooey said. "But I can't come to your party."

"You haven't even asked your mom yet. I know she's strict with you, but she'll let you come to *this* party."

"It's not my mom!" Zooey burst out. Lily could imagine her cheeks burning bright red, her eyes popping wide open.

"Then what's the problem?"

"I can't tell you!" Zooey said, and she just hung up with a click in Lily's ear.

Lily considered it for a few seconds and then shrugged. Sometimes Zooey got funky. It probably was about her mom and she didn't want to admit it, since Lily's mom was so cool about letting her give parties and stuff. With that in mind, Lily gathered up her journal and pen and headed for the family room.

Dad was in his chair, glasses perched at the end of his nose, studying a battered copy of some C. S. Lewis book.

Mom had volleyball camp registration forms spread out and was frowning at them, a pencil parked over her ear.

"Can we talk about my party?" Lily asked.

Dad smiled up at her foggily from C. S. Lewis, nodded, and went back to reading.

"Your dad's listening," Mom said dryly. "Me too. Go for it."

Lily settled herself on a floor cushion and opened her journal.

"I want to invite thirty people. Here's an example of the invitation—of course, I'll want to use real towel material—this is just a dummy—and for food, a watermelon shell with fruit in it, a fruit and Cool Whip salad, chicken kabobs, hamburgers, hot dogs we'll cook on the grill later, and different kinds of chips.

"We'll need to get a kiddie pool to put ice and drinks in, and a beach umbrella for over that and a bunch more umbrellas to put around the yard. I'm thinking a giant basket for towels so they don't have to bring their own—that way they can be color-coordinated.

"Oh—my color scheme—citrus-fruit colors ... tangerine, grapefruit, lemon, lime. Okay, then, I want to do a lot with seashells—hang them in garlands, do a table decoration—"

"Lil—"

"Oh, and when they first walk in the door, I want a picnic basket full of beach stuff in the entrance hall—"

"Lily—"

"And I want to make big bare feet that lead people through the house to the back door—"

"Lilianna!"

Lily stopped. Dad even looked up from C. S. Lewis and took his glasses off.

"Do you have any idea how much all of that is going to cost?" Mom asked.

"Well, no," Lily said. "But you said I could have a party."

"I said a party, not the inaugural ball. Your father and I didn't go that all-out for our wedding."

"I don't remember beach balls at our wedding, that's true," Dad said.

"I just want it to be the ultimate party," Lily said.

"But we can't afford ultimate." Mom said. "What about mildly great?"

Lily pulled loose a curl of red hair and stretched it out so she could frown at it. Her stomach was sinking again.

"I can see that doesn't excite you," Mom said. "But—"

"Before we start 'butting,'" Dad said, "what about this idea?"

Lily held her breath. The last time he'd come up with an idea it was to invite his mother to stay with them through eternity.

He said, "What if we give you a certain amount of money for your party, just like we did for the boys' activities, and then you earn the rest yourself? Joe recycled everything in the known world. Art mowed lawns."

"And what's Lil going to do?" Mom said. "It's a little scary, if you ask me."

"Mo-om!" Lily wailed.

"I'm sorry," Mom said. "I couldn't resist that."

"What do you say, Lilliputian?" Dad said.

"Yes," Lily said. "There's a lot of stuff I can do to earn money."

"Atta girl," Dad said.

"But keep it simple, Lil," Mom said. "You don't have to form a nonprofit corporation."

Lily fell asleep that night imagining herself acting as a nanny to children like Anne of Green Gables did before she got adopted, or starting a nursery school in the backyard like Louisa May Alcott did.

But the next morning the best opportunity of all presented itself right in the front yard—with its head in the garbage can.

Chapter 4

Lily was just about to turn on the *Home and Garden* channel when she heard a clanging noise outside. It sounded like somebody had put a bunch of tin cans in a dryer.

She set her bowl of Cheerios on the coffee table and went through the living room to look out the front window. There was garbage all over the driveway—soup cans, mayonnaise jars, banana peels, and coffee grounds still stuck to their filters. The big Rubbermaid trash can was still partly upright, and all Lily could see left in it was the bottom half of a large black dog. The stub of a tail was wiggling back and forth as if whatever rotted delicacy he had found was making him very happy.

Lily pulled open the front door and went out on the porch in her bare feet and Garfield T-shirt.

"Hey—you!" she called out in a loud whisper. "Get out of there!"

The tail stopped, and the legs backed up. A wide head pulled itself out of the trash can and turned to look casually at Lily. It was the Woods' rottweiler.

"Go home!" Lily hissed.

*Get lost,* the dog seemed to answer. He dove back into the trash can. Lily padded down the steps and hurried toward him.

"Hey," she said when she reached his backside. "Get out of there!"

She gave the rottweiler's rear a poke, and once again he backed out, this time with an old, charred hot dog in his mouth. Lily gagged.

"That is so gross!" she said. "Drop it—come on—drop it!"

She tapped his nose. He blinked and let the hot dog drop to the ground with the rest of the garbage. Lily reached down to grab his collar. He slurped the side of her face with his tongue.

"Gross me out and make me icky!" she said.

She scrubbed at her cheek with the back of her free hand. "You are *so* going home!" she told him.

That seemed fine with him, though as he let her lead him down the driveway by the collar, he did look longingly at the dropped hot dog.

"Forget it, pal," Lily said. "You've had your breakfast."

When Lily knocked on the Woods' door, Mrs. Woods answered wearing hot rollers and carrying her baby boy on her hip. He was wailing and smearing the contents of a runny nose all over his face.

"Your dog got out," Lily said.

"Is that—did he?"

"Yeah," Lily said.

"I am *so* sorry."

"It's okay," Lily said. By now the baby had snot in his hair. This lady had enough problems.

"I can't keep him in the yard," Mrs. Woods said, bouncing her baby. "He needs more exercise than he's getting, but with the baby sick, I just don't have time to walk him."

The idea came into Lily's head fully formed. "I could walk him for you," Lily said. "I wouldn't even charge you that much."

Mrs. Woods looked down at the rottweiler sitting next to her, licking cereal off the baby's toes. "You did handle him great," she said. "He let you bring him right home."

*Was that so surprising?* Lily wondered. They'd never had a dog at their house. She wasn't sure how dogs were supposed to act.

The baby let out an ear-piercing scream, and the rottweiler tried to wriggle out the door. Lily grabbed him, and Mrs. Woods sighed.

"All right," she said. "I'll pay you ten bucks a week if you'll take him for a walk every night after supper. Fair enough?"

"Definitely!" Lily said. "I'll see you tonight!"

She raced across the street already calculating. Ten dollars a week for the five weeks between now and the party—

"That's fifty bucks!" she told her mom a few minutes later. Lily followed her around the room while she gathered up her stuff.

"It's a good start," Mom said. "Has anybody seen my sunglasses?"

"Good start?" Lily said.

"That ought to cover a couple of beach umbrellas or a kiddie pool full of sodas. Here they are, right where I left them." She gave Lily one of her twitchy smiles as she put on her sunglasses. "Get a couple more dog-walking jobs to go with that one, and you might be able to set the party table. Either that, or you need to pare your plans down a little."

*No way,* Lily thought as Mom grabbed her lunch and headed for the door. *I'm going to have the ultimate party if I have to walk fifty dogs at once!*

She scrambled upstairs and in about two hours' time, she'd made up ten flyers, each with a drawing of a different kind of dog on it. They all said *Lily's Dog-Walking Service* with her phone number and fee of two dollars an hour printed in large red letters. She was rummaging in a kitchen drawer for masking tape when Joe came in, sticking his ball cap on over uncombed hair.

"What's this?" he said, picking up a flyer. "It looks like you're going to walk a cow."

Lily snatched it back from him. "It's a Scottie dog."

"Who's got a Scottie dog?"

"Nobody!"

"Then how are you gonna walk one if nobody's got one?"

"Somebody might—oh, just shut up!"

She picked up the whole stack of flyers, jammed the roll of masking tape onto her wrist like a bracelet, and stomped out of the kitchen.

"Did you ever walk a dog before?" Joe called after her.

*Yeah!* Lily thought angrily. *Just this morning.*

That bothered her a little—the fact that she didn't have much, well, *any*, experience walking dogs. But it didn't keep people from hiring her. Every time she knocked on a door or caught a dog owner about to leave for work in her car, she told them Mrs. Woods had hired her to walk her rottweiler. They all said something like, "Well, if you can handle that animal, you can probably handle mine," and by mid-morning she'd covered the block and had five more customers.

She was smiling to herself a half hour later when she'd finished punching the numbers into Art's calculator. In five weeks, she was going to have three hundred dollars.

*Silly teenagers don't make three hundred dollars, Mudda,* she thought smugly. And then she spent the rest of the day making a shopping list.

She also called the Girlz and told them—or their answering machines—that next week she'd have enough money to buy the stuff for the decorations and invitations and they could come over and help her make them. By then there wasn't time to even say hi to Mom and Dad when they got home because she had to take care of her first clients.

"You don't know how glad I am you showed up today," said Mr. Glodowski around the corner when Lily arrived. "These mutts are about to drive me batty. My wife's with our daughter—she just had a baby. These dogs are worse than any kid we ever had. 'Course, they do have pedigrees. They've cost me more than my kids did."

Mr. Glodowski kept mumbling into his mustache as he led Lily toward the laundry room. When he opened the door, two large masses of curly, black hair hurled themselves at Lily, yipping and licking and panting like they'd just run a marathon. But wild as they were, they worked like an organized team. One put his paws on Lily's shoulders and held her against the wall while the other one made repeated lunges to lick Lily's nose, ears, and eyebrows.

"What kind of dogs are these?" Lily managed to ask between slurps.

"Standard poodles," Mr. Glodowski said as he produced a pair of perfectly matched leather leashes. "Chloe! Pierre! Heel!"

Mr. Glodowski hooked a leash onto Pierre's collar and handed the other one to Lily. Luckily, Chloe was so busy digging her tongue into Lily's inner ear she didn't notice she was being tethered.

"Looks like you've got a good handle on them," Mr. Glodowski said. "Keep them out as long as you want—I'll even pay you extra. Take them out for a hamburger—I don't care—just don't let anything happen to them. My wife would kill me."

"Oh, don't worry," Lily said, hopping over the leashes as Pierre and Chloe began to dance their way toward the door. "I've got everything under control."

She smiled her biggest smile at Mr. Glodowski until he grinned back and faded off into his den. Then Lily looked down at the two dogs attempting the tango at leash ends.

"All right, you two," she said. "We're going for a walk."

Both curled, coifed heads came up like pieces of toast popping up in a toaster. Suddenly, the tango was over and a jitterbug began as they dug their toenails into the linoleum trying to get to the door. Lily got the thing open and was immediately pulled down the back steps, across the yard, and around to the front. By the time they reached the sidewalk, her arm felt like it had been pulled out of the socket. It was time to take charge, just like she'd done with the rottweiler.

"Wait a minute!" she shouted at them. "You are *so* not pulling me down the street! I'm pulling *you!*"

But they did yet another pirouette around each other and took off down the sidewalk with Lily flying out behind.

*Well, they* are *French poodles,* she thought. *Maybe they don't speak English.*

"Wait!" she shouted as they hauled her off. "I'll get you a croissant!"

They obviously weren't interested in food or anything else except dragging Lily down the street. The only good thing she could think of was that none of her other customers lived down this way to see her.

"You guys—stop!" she shouted at the poodles.

Chloe sprang off to the left after a passing dragonfly, and Pierre lunged to the right where a squirrel was obviously calling his name. Lily suddenly felt like a zipper being yanked open. If she didn't let go of one of them soon—

She didn't have to make a decision. As the taunting squirrel ran up an oak tree, Pierre gave a yelp—which was clearly in French—and leaped after it. The leash tore out of Lily's hand.

But there was no time to take off after Pierre, because Chloe was doubling her efforts to get to the dragonfly, and without her brother pulling from the other direction, she was now able to drag Lily right along with her.

Lily grabbed at Chloe's leash with both hands as she bawled out, "Heel! Heel, Chloe!" It hadn't worked for Mr. Glodowski, either, so she shut up and hung on as Chloe hauled her across the street. As the dog dug in like a racehorse toward the park on the other side of the street, she took Lily with her over the curb.

Lily's sneaker caught the edge of the concrete and she was suddenly horizontal, hands still clinging to the leash, belly bouncing over the sidewalk and across the grass.

"Chlo-*eee!*" Lily screamed. But Chloe was now moving at a dead gallop, dodging swing sets and barely missing monkey bars. Still jouncing and bumping on the ground on her stomach, Lily had to close her eyes to keep them from filling with the dirt Chloe was kicking up with her back paws.

Bad move. Somewhere between the sandbox and the jungle gym, Chloe cut it a little too close. With her eyes squeezed shut, Lily didn't see the bench coming until Lily slid into it, ribs first. The leash ripped out of her hands, and as Lily opened her eyes, she saw Chloe disappearing in a cloud of dust.

"No! Stop—you evil dog!" Lily screamed at her.

She tried to scramble up, but she was under the seat of the bench, and by the time she could crawl out, retrieve the tennis shoe that had flown off in the crash, and spit the dirt out of her mouth, Chloe was long gone.

And there was no telling where Pierre was by now, or what was going to happen when Mr. Glodowski found out his wife's prize pedigrees were missing. Thoughts started pushing, shoving, and colliding in Lily's head so hard she had to close her eyes again and put both hands on her temples to settle them down. She heard a horn blow.

*Oh, please, God, don't let that be Mr. Glodowski.*

"Hey, Lily. What are you doin'?" somebody yelled from the direction of the car horn.

It was worse than Mr. Glodowski. It was Art.

Lily opened her eyes. He had pulled the Subaru—Ruby Sue—up to the curb and was leaning out the window on the passenger side, face scrunched up into a question mark.

"What happened to you?" Art asked. "Come 'ere."

"I can't," Lily said. "I gotta go find—"

"You gotta go find a doctor. Dude, look at your leg."

Art's face pulled out of its question mark and into what looked like concern. Lily's eyes followed his down to her knee. Blood trickled down her leg, ready to trail into her sock at any moment.

She swiped at it with her hand and looked around once more for signs of Chloe. There were none. Beyond her, the car door slammed and Art came toward her.

"Are you in trouble?" he said.

"Are you gonna tell?" she said.

"Depends."

"On what?"

"On what kinda trouble. Did somebody, like, try to mug you or something?"

"No—" Lily said.

"Did you try to mug somebody else?"

"No!"

"Then I probably won't tell. What's goin' on?"

Lily spilled it all. Then she waited for Art's sarcastic comment and maybe a ride home, where she would face groundation for a good two weeks—not to mention the wrath of Mr. Glodowski.

"So let's go find the dogs," Art said.

Lily stared at him. He wasn't smirking. He *was* looking at her like she was the ditsiest person since Ronald McDonald, but he was also jerking his head toward Ruby Sue.

"Come on," he said. "How far could they have gotten?"

"You really think we can find them?" Lily finally managed to say.

"Not if we stand here, we won't. Get in the car. Let's cruise."

Chapter 5

For the first two blocks, Lily hung out the car window shouting, "Chloe! Pierre!" until Art threatened to call off the whole mission if she didn't get her head back in the car and stop acting like an escapee from a psychiatric ward.

Lily looked glumly out the window as they turned the corner onto Summer Avenue, where the COPs—"cranky old people"—were pruning their hedge. Joe had called them that ever since they'd yelled at him for using that same hedge for a hurdle.

"Maybe we should ask them," Lily said.

"Oh, yeah, and maybe we should also invite somebody to rip our lips off. We'll just cruise," Art said. "They gotta show up sometime. They don't exactly blend with the environment. Who would want sissy dogs like that, anyway?"

"Not me," Lily said. In fact, she hoped she never *saw* another dog again in her entire life.

As it turned out, she didn't see another one, at least not for the next ten minutes. Art cruised Ruby Sue around every block for a one-mile radius, and there was no sign of either Chloe or Pierre. By the time they'd circled back to the park, Lily was chewing on her hair.

"Would you knock that off?" Art said to her. "It's gross."

"I can't help it!" Lily said. "If I don't find these dogs, my life is over."

"How much did you say they were worth?" Art said.

"More than their kids."

"Oh. Well, you could have a point then. Chew away."

Lily did, eyes glued to the houses, staring back at her.

"Maybe somebody's got them in their house!" she said suddenly.

"Look, I said I'd cruise you around. I'm not gonna go knockin' on doors."

"You don't have to do any knocking—just drive me," Lily said.

"Somebody's liable to call the cops on ya," Art said. "Okay—there's a guy—just ask him. Don't knock on any doors though, dude, that's—that's desperate."

"I *am* desperate!" Lily said.

*Please, God,* she prayed as Art pulled Ruby Sue over so she could get out at the house where a man was flipping hamburgers over a grill in his backyard. *Please—just help me find them!*

She swallowed guiltily as she approached the chain-link fence. She'd been spending more time searching the Bible for party ideas than doing what the book said to do, but she promised God right then that was going to change—as soon as she found those French poodles.

The man looked up from his burgers with a start when Lily said, "Um, hi. Have you seen two big poodles?"

He went back to the spatula. "I saw one," he said. "How could I miss it? It came sailing right over the fence into my yard."

"Do you still have her?" Lily said.

The man gave a grunt. "Not hardly. She jumped right out again. Over that way."

He jerked his head toward the other side of the yard.

"Did you see where she went?" Lily said.

"No. But I heard. Old Man Weiss started yelling his head off when it got to his place a couple doors down."

"Is that the cranky old—is that the guy with the hedges?"

"Yep. Dog probably knocked a petal off a rose or somethin'. Old Man Weiss doesn't like anybody messin' up his yard—especially dogs. They know him by his first name down at the pound."

"The *pound?*" Lily said. Her heart was halfway up her esophagus and thumping hard. "You think he called the pound?" Lily said.

"The paddy wagon went by here a couple minutes ago. Guy already had one yelpin' in the back, and that one joined right in. That's why I got cats—"

Lily didn't stay to hear about his felines. She tore back to Ruby Sue, hair slapping against her face in wet strands.

"They're at the pound!" she cried before she could even get the door open.

"We're there," Art said, and he gunned the motor even as Lily was piling in.

Burlington County Animal Shelter was the official name on the side of the building they pulled up to. It was obviously sheltering quite a few animals, because the sound of barking as they hurried up the steps was deafening. Lily never knew there were so many ways *to* bark. When she asked in a shaky voice at the front counter if any big French poodles had been brought in, the woman gave a prim nod.

"Yes," she said, giving Lily and Art a disapproving look. "We picked up one of them at a Mr. Weiss' house—"

"Those are the ones," Lily said breathlessly.

"At least you were obeying the leash law," the prim lady said. "But they did get away from you, didn't they?"

"They got away from *her,*" Art said, pointing to Lily.

The woman got up and led them toward the door where the yelping and yipping and snarling were coming from. "You need to get them under control," she said. "We offer obedience classes five times a week—absolutely free."

"We've tried obedience classes," Art said. "The girl's untrainable."

The lady gave Art a half smile. "I was talking about the dogs."

She took them into a large room lined with cages. Each one held at least three dogs—and every one of them was barking. The minute the hounds spotted the three of them, they took it up a notch.

"Do all these dogs belong to somebody?" Art shouted over the din.

"They did at some point," the lady said. "Except that poor thing. I don't think anybody would ever claim him." She pointed at a cage at the bottom and kept walking. "Your poodles are over here," she said, rounding the corner. "We gave them the deluxe suite."

It was just a bigger version of all the other cages, but it looked like the Ritz Carlton to Lily—because the two poodles were in it.

"You have to match the names on the tags," the lady said.

"Chloe and Pierre Glodowski," Lily said.

The lady stopped with her hand on the latch. "Now, do you think you can get them out to your car?"

"My brother'll take one," Lily said.

But when she turned around, Art wasn't there.

"Looks like you need a leash for him too," the lady said.

Lily strode down the hall and around the corner, where she stopped dead. There stood Art, cradling something gray and homely in his arms.

"What are you doing?" she said, marching up to him. "We have to get Pierre and Chloe back before Mr. Glodowski calls the cops."

"Look at this little dude," Art said. "Isn't he cool?"

Lily gave the dog a glance. He was skinny and wiry and was having a very bad hair day. Gray, wire-like curls stood up in the middle of his head like a Mohawk. The legs that dangled down from Art's arms looked too long. The eyes that stared back at her bugged out too much. The tail slapping against Art's shirt was too much like a broken-off twig to be considered anything but unattractive.

"Look at him," Art said. "He's sittin' here in the middle of all this, and he's just chillin'. This is a cool dog."

"Would you put him back?" Lily said. "We gotta get out of here."

"Feel him. Dude—he's, like, tough."

She ran a hand quickly over its head. Like the snapping of fingers, the dog whipped back and got Lily's hand between its teeth.

"Hey!" Lily said.

"He's just sayin' hi," Art said.

"He needs to learn some manners then," Lily said. She pried her fingers out of the dog's mouth and examined the teeth marks.

"He's a puppy," Art said.

"He's a freak. Put him back—we gotta get the poodles home."

A girl who worked there—this one a teenager in tight jeans and made-up eyes that flirted up at Art—took the puppy from him.

"You don't want to take him home?" she said.

"I'd love to take him home," Art said. "But my mom would probably have a cow."

"You could ask her," the girl said. "Or you could call her, and I could ask her for you."

Lily got Art by the arm before he could offer to take the *girl* with them. He was still drooling over his shoulder as they rounded the corner. Since when was Art into girls anyway?

Within minutes they had Pierre and Chloe on leashes and in the back seat of Ruby Sue. Both dogs behaved like teacher's pets in obedience school.

"Why couldn't you have acted like that for me?" she said to them as Art headed toward the Glodowski house.

"They're just wiped out from what they've been through," Art said. "Dude, I sure hate to see little Otto have to spend another night in that place."

"Who's Otto?" Lily said.

"That cool dog. I just named him that," Art said.

Mr. Glodowski met them at the car in front of his house, shaking his head.

"I just got a call from Old Man Weiss," he said as he ushered the now docile Chloe and Pierre out of the backseat. "Old grouch."

Lily resisted the urge to chew on her hair. "Should I come by tomorrow night?" she said.

"I don't think so," Mr. Glodowski said. "I'll just call if I can use you."

Lily fell into a miserable slump as they drove away.

"Aw, don't worry about it," Art said. "Those are sissy dogs anyway. Now, Otto—*that's* a dog."

"I don't ever want to hear the word *dog* again," Lily said.

But as she'd heard Mudda say many times, "Wanting isn't getting." By the time she got home, all five of her other customers had called wanting to know if she was going to show up, and four of them had canceled their order. Only Mrs. Woods was holding out for her rottweiler.

"I'll walk him tomorrow," Lily said. "What's for dinner?"

"Hot dogs," Mom said. "I'll keep some warmed up for you. Go. Meet your commitment."

"But I'm no good at this—"

"Keep your promises, Lily," Mom said, "or there will be no party."

*There isn't going to be much of one anyway,* Lily thought, trudging glumly toward the Woods' house. Fifty dollars, plus whatever Mom and Dad were giving her, wasn't going to produce much more than the lame graduation party had to offer.

*God, I'm sorry,* she thought, *but I think I hate my life right now. This couldn't get worse.*

But she had no idea what she was talking about—absolutely no idea.

Chapter 6

The Woods' rottweiler, whose name turned out to be Adolf, seemed to remember Lily. He slunk along beside her during the whole walk, except for when he stopped to sniff at people's garbage cans.

"Who needs dog food for you?" Lily said to him. "They could just feed you trash, and you'd be happy."

She walked Adolf until it was almost dark. She hoped supper would be over at home and she could take her plate up to her room and be miserable by herself. But when she got there, everybody was just sitting down. Art was going on and on about Otto.

"He's a totally lovable little guy," he said. "You wouldn't be able to resist him, Mom."

"Yes, you would," Lily said. "He tries to put his tongue in your mouth and up your nose—"

"Gross," Joe said.

"And when you push him away, he nips at you."

"He's just a pup though," Art said.

"Yeah, with teeth like knitting needles!"

"Dude, he needs love, that's all. Needs somebody to spend some time with him. You should see the way his little tail wags. He's just waiting for you to play with him."

"He's just waiting to devour you!" Lily said.

Mom and Dad were by this time exchanging looks across the table—looks that meant they were carrying on a conversation without saying a word. Joe was watching them.

"You're thinkin' about lettin' us get him, aren't you?" he said. "You *are!* That would be so cool to have a dog!"

"Let's back the truck up," Mom said. "Who exactly is going to spend all this quality time you say Otto needs so desperately?"

"Me!" Joe and Art said at the same time.

"Uh-huh," Mom said. "Need I remind you that you said the same thing about the turtles, and I found *them* gasping for their lives in a dry bowl *under* your bed." She arched an eyebrow at Joe.

"That was back when I was a kid!" Joe said.

"Besides," Art said, "turtles don't have personality. Otto—he's got enough for five or six dogs. He's tries to talk to ya. I'm serious. He's all growling and snarlin' at me, trying to get his point across."

"And his point *is* that he wants to bite your arm off," Lily said. "Mom, don't let him bring that mutt home. He's evil!"

"He's cool," Art said. "He's got these big brown eyes and these—expressive ears—"

"Good word," Dad said. He nodded at Mom as if Art had just scored several points for Otto with his vocabulary alone.

"And this is the killer," Art was saying. "Everything on him droops when he's sad. You should've seen him when we left—even his lower lip was hanging down, like he could hardly stand it."

"Yeah," Lily said, holding out her hand to display the teeth marks Otto had etched there. "He saw his lunch going out the door!"

"I'm telling you, the poor little guy is deprived. When you're holding him, he just can't get close enough to you. I thought he was gonna become one with my armpit."

"I'll say one thing," Mom said to Art. "I haven't seen you show tenderness like this for anybody or anything since you were in third grade. It's refreshing."

"I'm just being humane," Art said.

"Another excellent word," Dad said.

"Let's get back to the care and feeding of this beast," Mom said. She wiggled her finger back and forth between the boys. "Let's look at this realistically . . ."

"I know," Art said. "He's gotta be fed, walked, played with, brushed—"

"What about potty training?" Mom said.

Art shook his head. "Oh, he's old enough to be housebroken already. I don't think we have to worry about that."

"A minute ago when I was talking about him trying to chew my arm to shreds, he was just a puppy!" Lily said.

"Oh, I forgot to tell you, Joe," Art said. "He's got this cool little goatee." He stroked his chin. "It made me think I might wanna grow one."

"So, he's a mixed breed," Dad said. "You know, mongrel dogs are usually a lot less trouble than your purebreds." Dad looked sympathetically at Lily. "Pedigreed dogs can be high-strung; no wonder those poodles got away from you."

"Yeah, and I was *wishing* this Otto dog would get away from me," Lily said. "But, Dad, he hooked his teeth around my finger."

"You wouldn't have to even touch him or go near him, Lily," Art said.

"Yeah," Joe said. "Me and Art'll be the ones takin' care of him."

"Art and I," Dad said.

Joe looked a little stung. "You could help too, Dad, but I wanna do some stuff. Dude, I always wanted a dog."

45

"So I'm hearing you say you'll take total charge of Otto's care," Mom said.

"Yeah!" the boys said together.

There was another wordless discussion between Mom and Dad.

"All right, then," Dad said finally. "Otto joins the family, but with the stipulation that you characters—" he pointed to Joe and Art—"do everything for him."

"And I want that in writing," Mom said. But the corners of her mouth were twitching, and nobody went for pad and pencil.

*It doesn't matter,* Lily told herself firmly. *It's between Mom and Dad and them—so what do I care? I have enough to worry about with my party.*

She spent the whole next day, when she wasn't walking Adolf, making modified invitations. Since she couldn't afford color-coordinated towels, she got Mom's permission to cut up a bunch of her old ones into mini-beach towels, then used tee-shirt paint to write the time and date and all the other important information on each one. It took hours, but when she was finished and had them spread out all over the family room to dry, she started to get excited about the party again.

Lily was looking fondly at the invitations when the door from the garage to the kitchen was flung open. For a few seconds, all Lily heard was a ticking sound on the kitchen floor. By the time she heard Art call out, "Here, Otto! Come on, boy!" it was too late.

Toenails slid crazily across the hardwood dining room floor, and Otto was suddenly in the doorway to the family room, gray fur standing up on his head. His brown eyes took in the room at a glance, and his ears went up and out like he was about to take off in flight. Lily wished he had. Before she could even open her mouth, he'd charged into the room.

"No, Otto!" she screamed.

Otto headed straight for her. Between them was the spread of thirty mini beach towels with wet paint on them. Lily tried to untangle her legs to get up, but Otto already had all four paws planted on the first row of invitations and was headed for the second.

Only, the first set was still clinging to him as he pranced on. He whirled around to inspect what was happening, catching three more invitations with his tail. His nose went down, straight into Ashley's, and he came up with it attached to his nose.

"No, you evil dog!" Lily screamed.

"Don't yell at him!" Art screamed just as loudly from the doorway.

Otto's expressive ears dropped as if he'd been smacked, and he made three complete circles in a spasm of fear, picking up several more tiny, paint-wet beach towels as he twirled.

"Make him stop it!" Lily shouted at Art as she tried to grab the last few invitations that hadn't been trampled on. She managed to grab one, but Otto hurled himself past her and plastered it against the front of her shirt.

"Art! *Do* something!" she cried.

"Come here, Otto!" Art called out, tramping over what was left of the little towels toward the couch the puppy had just dived behind. "Come on, boy. It's all right."

"It's *not* all right! Look what he did!"

Art seemed to care less about the fact that a whole afternoon's work was now either smeared all over the carpet or stuck on the fur of a dog that still hadn't finished plowing a path through the family room. Just as Art got himself wedged behind the couch, Otto squirmed out the other end and leaped up onto Dad's chair, a piece of faded blue terrycloth still hanging from his nose by a glob of fluorescent yellow paint.

"Come here, you little brat!" Lily cried.

"Don't yell at him!" Art hollered. "You're freakin' him out!"

Otto sprang off the chair in the direction of the coffee table.

Lily lunged for the table to rescue the tubes of puffy paint, but not before Otto planted one paw firmly on the hot pink and sent it spurting straight across the room, directly onto the TV screen.

Otto didn't stop to survey his artwork. He trounced over two more tubes and took yet one more flying leap—into Lily's arms. His towel-bedecked, painted muzzle went into her neck, and he stayed there, quivering. He felt like a trembling fist against her chest.

"Get him off of me," Lily said through gritted teeth.

"Come on, boy," Art said.

But when he put his hands on the puppy's sides, Otto let out a low growl between his *own* gritted teeth.

"No, dude, it's me," Art said.

But another gentle tug by Art just got him another snarl. Otto squirmed to get closer to Lily's neck.

"Let go of him," Art said.

"I'm barely touching him! Take him!"

When Art tried, Otto snapped at Art's index finger. Art drew back with a yelp that sounded a lot like Otto himself.

"It doesn't hurt," Lily said, teeth still clenched. "He's just a puppy."

"Shut up," Art said. "Dude, what's the matter with him?"

"I don't care!" Lily said. "Look what he did to my invitations!"

She dumped Otto onto the couch and looked down at the devastation at her feet. "I spent hours doing these—and I used all the old towels—and I don't have money to buy more stuff! I hate dogs!"

"Uh-oh," Art said. "Look."

Lily turned around in time to see Otto coming back up from a squat. There was now a wet spot on the couch cushion.

"Dude, that's not good," Art said. "We gotta get that cleaned up before Mom gets home, or she'll make him go back to the pound."

"I thought you said he was potty trained."

Art ignored her and reached once more for Otto. "First I gotta put him out in the garage before he does that again, and then—"

But Otto pranced backwards on the couch and snarled, showing his rows of little canines under curled lips.

"I hate to tell you this," Lily said, "but I don't think he likes you."

"He's just scared, and who can blame him? He's not in the house two minutes and you've got him all painted up like a clown. What *is* all this stuff, anyway?"

Lily glared at him. "It *was* my party invitations. Now it's tomorrow's trash."

"Oh," Art said.

"Yeah, oh—so could you get your stupid dog out of here?"

Art gave Otto a dubious look. "I'm your pal, dude," he said to the dog. "I'm the one who saved you from the pound, remember?"

He leaned toward Otto. The puppy went into another fit of toothy barking and then threw himself back into Lily's arms. The piece of towel came off his nose and dropped face down on the table.

"*I'm* taking him out to the garage!" Lily said. "And I'm never letting him back in!"

She parked Otto outside the door and ignored his puppified howling as she headed back for the family room to survey the damages. They were worse than she thought. There wasn't a single invitation that was still fit to send out, and there was barely a spot in the room that hadn't been touched by dog hair or puffy paint.

Lily and Art had barely finished cleaning it all up and were still fighting over who should have to pay for her to make new invitations when Mom came in the front door with Joe.

"What is all that carrying on?" she said.

"It's the puppy!" Joe cried, and tore for the door.

"You can't just put him in the garage and forget about him," Mom said. Her eyes trailed around the family room. "Did you guys clean this room? Quick, let me write this down someplace."

"We *had* to clean," Lily started to say.

49

But she was cut off by a yelp from the direction of the back door. Joe reappeared, eyes indignant.

"That dog snapped at me!" he said.

"He's still scared," Art said. "Everything's new to him."

"He isn't going to get acquainted standing out there," Mom said. "Bring him in."

"Lily, bring him in," Art said.

"Me?" Lily said. "I'd rather be shot."

"You're the only one he hasn't tried to bite since he got here."

"Do it, Lil, just this once, would you?" Mom said. "I can't take much more of that crying. Don't they make pacifiers for puppies?"

*How about my fist down his little throat?* Lily thought as she marched angrily to the back door. *If he bites me, so help me, I'm going to go feed him to Adolf.*

But when she reached down to grab Otto by the scruff of the neck, he didn't growl. He flipped himself around, scrambled into Lily's arms, and began a thorough licking of the side of her face.

"Gross me out and make me icky!" she cried, and hauled him into the house. "You're Art's dog, have you got that? You're not mine!"

# Chapter 7

Lily must have told Otto that a dozen times over the next several days, but he slept in her bed every night, burrowing himself under the covers like a mole and licking between her toes every time he woke up, which was in intervals of twenty minutes.

He wouldn't eat his food out of his bowl unless Lily put it in there for him and stood next to him while he ate it. If Art or Joe or even Mom or Dad tried to do it, he did his little back-up dance and barked and snarled until Mom said, "Lil, please feed him before I flush him down the toilet."

Lily would gladly have let her do it. After all, when he finished gobbling down his Puppy Chow, he usually went immediately up to her room and chewed up something of hers. When he devoured the tangerine-colored sandals she'd talked Mom into buying her for the party, Lily was headed with him in her arms for the bathroom. He seemed to sense his doom though and wriggled away to hide in the laundry basket.

She thought the worst of it was when he decided "their" bedroom was also his bathroom and deposited a smelly pile right next to the bed. When Lily wound up with poo between her toes, she screamed until the entire Robbins family came rushing to the room, even Joe. He, of course, rolled in the hallway laughing when he saw her feet.

"You won't think it's so funny when it happens to you!" Lily said to him. "Tonight, he sleeps in your room!"

Joe was up for that. Otto wasn't. Even when Joe smuggled a whole hamburger into his room for Otto's bedtime snack, the puppy stood inside the door and wailed until Mom finally told Lily to let him sleep in her room one more time. Lily awoke before dawn to see Mom trying to coax Otto out with a piece of steak to get him to go potty outside before he produced another prize for Lily. Otto was ignoring the steak and snarling fiercely at Mom.

"I'll do it, Mom," Lily said sleepily. "Do you know how much I hate this dog?"

"Can we use another word besides 'hate'?" Mom said.

"How about despise?"

"That works."

But if Lily thought getting up before the sun every morning of her summer to take her brother's dog out was the worst—she hadn't seen anything. The worst, it seemed to her, happened the day the Girlz came over to help her start on the party decorations. She'd at last gotten her first week's pay from Mrs. Woods and finally found a time when everybody was free. They could at least get started on the papier-mâché sand castles for the tables.

It wasn't going that well even before Otto came on the scene. Reni got there first, and Lily showed her the magazine.

"What's this supposed to be?" Reni said, poking at the food picture with her finger.

"It's a sea-turtle salad," Lily said. "Isn't that cool?"

"Uh-huh. Um, Lil, are you really gonna put these little umbrella things in everybody's sodas?"

"Yeah. I told you—it's a beach theme. Every ultimate party has a theme."

"Okay," Reni said. "But don't wig out when Shad and those guys make fun of it."

"You think they will?" Lily said.

"I *know* they will. They'll say it's cheesy. I can hear 'em now."

Lily widened her eyes at Reni. "Do *you* think it's cheesy?"

"No way!" Reni said. "I'm just warning you, that's all. We better get started on your decorations. I can't stay that long. I gotta practice."

The ringing phone interrupted her. It was Zooey.

"I'm not coming," she said. Her voice was thick with tears.

"Why?" Lily said.

"Because my mom said if I'm not going to the party then I can't come help with the decorations."

"But she's the one who won't let you come to the party!"

"Yes, she will."

"Then why aren't you coming?"

"I just can't," Zooey sobbed and hung up.

"Does anybody know what's wrong with Zooey?" Lily said when she got back to the kitchen.

By then Kresha was there, and she turned her eyes deliberately to the stack of newspapers on the table.

"Vhat these for, Lee-lee?" she said, too cheerfully.

Lily narrowed her eyes at her. "You know what's up with Zooey, don't you?" she said. "Tell me!"

Kresha drew her finger across her lips like she was zipping a zipper.

"You can't make her tell if she's promised not to," Suzy said.

"Oh, never mind," Lily said. "Help me carry this stuff outside, would you? My mom says it's too messy for in here."

As it turned out, it was too messy for the backyard too. Lily mixed the glue from starch and water and flour, just the way the magazine said to, and Reni set up the cardboard boxes they were using for bases. Kresha was asking a million questions, and Suzy was patiently trying to answer them, when Otto woke up from the nap he was taking under a hydrangea bush and bolted toward Lily like a streak of lightning in a flea collar.

"No, Otto, get back!" she cried.

She only had one hand to ward him off with. The other was attached to a wooden spoon that was dunked in paste. Otto naturally went for the spoon-laden one. His paw hit the end of the handle, and thick, white paste catapulted out of the bowl and into Reni's hair.

"Hey!" she cried. "What *is* that gunk?"

"It's just glue—Otto—no!"

But it was too late. Otto already had the spoon locked firmly in his jaws and was tearing across the yard with it. Behind him, the bowl had landed on its side on top of the pile of newspapers, oozing starchy glue through every page and down the side of the picnic table.

"That's all the newspapers I had!" Lily wailed.

"What about my hair?" Reni said. "This stuff is drying fast."

"He's digging a hole under a rosebush," Suzy said nervously.

"He going to bury dat spoon," Kresha said.

Otto fooled them all. As they watched in horror, he bounded straight for the pool with the spoon still in his mouth, raining paste in his wake. He wiggled himself into the air and dropped into the water with room to spare.

By then the Girlz were too hysterical to even move. Lily stomped to the pool and leaned over the edge. Otto was dog paddling so fast, she could barely see his legs, and the gooey spoon was still in place between his teeth.

"Come here, you little monster!" Lily said.

He swam obediently to her, and she grabbed for him. Her fingers curled around the spoon, and before she could let go, Otto had taken off again. Her feet came off the ground and her face went forward into the water. She was almost all the way in when Suzy and Reni hauled her out by her ankles.

"I get the dog!" Kresha was shouting.

"I wouldn't use that," Suzy said.

"Use what?" Lily asked—and then she saw.

Kresha was pelting the still-paddling Otto with cardboard boxes— the same cardboard boxes Lily was going to use to build sand castles.

"Let's glue that dog's mouth shut," Reni said. "Lily, this is *never* gonna come out of my hair. It's sticking straight out. What's in it?"

"Just water and flour, "Lily said, "—and starch."

Reni let out a scream and ran for the phone. Suzy went after her, saying, "I think I can get it out, Reni." Lily turned to Kresha, who was watching Otto circle the pool amid the soggy, sinking boxes, blowing air out of his nose.

"Mouth already glue shut," Kresha said.

"Come here, Otto," Lily said. "I won't flush you down the toilet, I promise."

Otto paddled over. He had a strange look in his eyes.

Lily grabbed onto the wooden spoon and pulled. Otto came with it. She put her finger in his mouth and tried to pry it open. Kresha was right. He'd glued himself shut.

In spite of the temptation to leave him that way, Lily did call her dad, who came home to take her and Otto to the vet. The vet had to give Otto a shot to calm him down before he could work on him, and even then the doctor couldn't come near him unless Lily was holding him.

"Dad, can't we give him away or something?" Lily said on the way home as Otto slept, dopey and exhausted, in her lap.

"You do have a point, Lilliputian," Dad said. "Maybe we ought to talk to your mom about that, do you think?"

She did think that. But it didn't happen. What happened was that when they got home, Mudda's car was in the driveway, and Art and Joe were hauling two enormous suitcases into the house.

"Well, I guess she took me at my word," Dad said. "Looks like she's staying at least a month."

Lily had never felt so much like crying—until she got in the house, still carrying a groggy Otto, and her grandmother greeted her from the kitchen with "Come help me get this supper on the table, Lilianna. Since you're the only one not working around here, it's you and I at the stove."

Lily was tempted to hightail it up the stairs, but Mudda appeared in the dining room wiping her hands on her apron. Lily was sure she was the only woman left in the world who wore an apron.

Her grandmother's hair was in its usual tidy helmet, and although her face was reddish from being near the oven, her eyes were cool and direct as she looked at Lily.

"Do you always leave a mess like that on the patio when you go out?" she said.

"It was an emergency!" Lily said.

She looked down at Otto. He was wide awake, and his lip was starting to curl. Lily could feel the growl starting in his tight little belly.

"That's just what you needed to add to the chaos, Paul," Mudda said. "Could you have found a homelier one?"

Otto reared his iguana-like head back and barked—and barked—and barked yet again.

"Why don't you go get him settled down, Lilliputian?" Dad said. "I'll help your grandmother in the kitchen."

"No, you won't," Mudda said as they trailed off together. "We at least want this meal to be edible. Where does Joanna keep her wooden spoons? I don't know how she finds a thing in here."

The minute she disappeared into the kitchen, Otto stopped barking. Lily looked down at the ridge of hair on top of his head.

*Maybe we shouldn't get rid of you just yet after all,* she thought.

But the next week proved that even Otto was no match for Mudda. Of course, nobody else had to be. Mom, Dad, Art, and Joe were gone all day. After the first couple of mornings, Otto took to crawling under Lily's bed until Mudda went out at lunchtime to work in the garden. Then he would wriggle out and climb into Lily's lap, licking her face as if to say, "What happened to the good old days?"

The only good thing that came out of it was that Otto was house-broken within six hours of Mudda's arrival. The rest was enough to drive *Lily* under the bed.

In the first place, Mudda got her up at seven o'clock so she wouldn't miss the best part of the day. Lily didn't see what was so "best" about sitting on the patio staring into a cup of tea with milk.

Then Mudda made her eat enough breakfast to feed most of Art's jazz band—eggs, bacon, toast, and fruit. It wasn't so bad when she was getting away with feeding half of it to Otto, but when Mudda caught her, Otto was banished from the kitchen.

After breakfast, Mudda gave Lily her daily lesson in housekeeping. She had Lily cleaning things she never even knew they had. She pretty much kept her mouth shut at first, just to avoid Mudda's tight-lipped lectures. But the day Mudda had her wiping out the inside of the dish-washer, she couldn't hold back any longer.

"Maybe I'm a slow learner," Lily said, "but doesn't the soap and water clean this out when you run the dishes?"

Mudda looked up from the screws she had taken out of the light switch cover and was polishing with brass polish. "Where did you get that sarcastic tone?" she said. "We are going to get rid of that, posthaste."

Once the particular area Mudda wanted to concentrate on each day was clean enough to perform surgery in, they moved on to what Mudda referred to as "those essentials they don't teach you young girls anymore." Lily would rather have kept cleaning the toilets.

She had to practice her handwriting since according to Mudda it presently looked like "chicken scratching."

She had to start a journal of everything she read, and she had to read something to write in it every day. That wouldn't have been so bad, the reading part, because Lily loved to get lost in a book. But "lost" didn't *begin* to describe how she felt when she was struggling through *Pilgrim's Progress*.

Mudda even made her learn the "correct way" to serve tea. One afternoon, Lily knew she would split a seam if she drank one more drop of Earl Grey. Mudda insisted they keep on until she got it right.

"This isn't difficult, Lilianna," she said. "I don't know why you're fighting it so."

*Uh—because it's lame!* Lily said in her mind. *And I've got better things to do!*

"Am I going to receive an answer, or just sullen silence?" Mudda said.

"What does 'sullen' mean?" Lily said.

"That won't work as a diversionary tactic. You can look it up later."

"What does 'diversionary'—"

"I can see we're going to have to add vocabulary development to our list," Mudda said.

*I hope that doesn't mean you're staying another month,* Lily thought.

"Lilianna, you still haven't answered my question."

"Which question?"

"You have to learn to focus on what people are saying if you want to be a decent conversationalist. It isn't all about talking, you know. It's just as important to know how to listen."

*And you would know this how?*

"Your grandfather had a talent for including everyone at his table in the conversation. He was a master—it was an art with him. I'd like to see you develop that same skill. Though how it's going to happen at the dinner table in this house, I'm at a loss to know. No one listens to a thing anyone else is saying."

Lily tried a smile. "With Joe and Art, there usually isn't much that's worth listening to."

"You exclude yourself from that? All I've heard out of you since I got here has been party, party, party."

Lily could feel herself bristling. "That's me—the party animal," she said.

"Watch your tone," Mudda said.

After that, Lily decided it was safer to stick with sullen silence.

# Chapter 8

There were only two things keeping Lily from bursting out of her sullen silence. One was the party plans. Mudda let her have two hours to herself every afternoon while she took what she referred to as her quiet time. Lily scooted into her room—with Otto—and broke out the party journal and the copy of the 1970 *Family Circle*.

By the time Mudda had been there a week, Lily hadn't made much progress. She'd tried several different ways to make invitations—drawing beach balls, trying to stuff little notes into seashells from vacations gone by, cutting starfish out of old sponges. They were all a flop.

The decorations weren't going any better. A search through the attic, with some help from Kresha, who was the only one available, turned up some faded crepe paper. That was no thanks to Kresha, who was more interested in the trunks of old junk and clothes nobody had ever gotten around to sorting through.

Lily looked at her, dressed up in a green-and-yellow plaid sport coat and pinstriped bell-bottoms, and shook her head.

"Enjoy it while you can," she said. "If my grandmother ever sees this attic, she'll have me up here sorting it all out with her so fast—" Lily shuddered and picked up the two rolls of crepe paper. "How can I use these for a beach theme?"

The question was never answered. She put the crepe paper down to keep looking, and Otto grabbed it and had it chewed into confetti before Kresha or Lily caught him.

It was good that she had the Bible study Mom had her working on. At first it had been a good excuse to look for parties in the Old Testament. But one day she found something else that applied.

She was supposed to read about Job, and she got so into it, she didn't stop with the few chapters that were assigned for each day. The poor guy had so many horrible things happen to him, he reminded her of herself. She groaned with him over every sore, every death, and every dried-up plant in his fields. Some of his diseases grossed her out (and made her icky), but she hung in there with him. Like her, nobody understood what he was going through.

"I feel that way too, pal," she said one day.

Otto immediately turned from the empty paper-towel roll he was decimating—a word she learned from Dad when Otto destroyed the earpiece on his glasses—and perked up his ears.

"I wasn't talking to you," Lily said. "I was talking to Job."

Didn't matter to Otto. He abandoned the roll and jumped up on the bed, where he sniffed curiously at the Bible.

"Chew that and I *will* kill you," Lily said.

Otto rested his nose on the page and looked innocent.

"It isn't right, you know," she told him. "Everybody else is getting to do whatever they want, and here I am, being all good, hanging out with Mudda so nobody else has to, trying to earn my own money. Taking care of you—"

She poked a finger at his chest. He hooked his teeth around her finger but didn't sink them in.

"So what did Job do about it? I gotta read on and find out. Move, Otto."

He refused to, until she laid back, put him on her chest, and rested the book on top of him. He closed his eyes and started to snore.

Job's friends weren't much help. All they did was tell him he must have done something to make God mad or all this stuff wouldn't be happening. But nobody could come up with anything Job had ever done wrong.

Lily got all the way to the end of the book, and Job was still wasting away with running sores, and practically everybody he loved had been killed off. Finally, he got it.

It was all about God—trusting God—knowing God has something in mind and that he'll come through for you if you just keep hanging in there. When Job did that, everything fell back into place, better than before.

Lily sat straight up on the bed, knocking Otto off onto the bedspread. He grumbled under his breath and rearranged himself against Lily's big stuffed panda, China.

"I'm gonna do that," Lily said to him. "I'm gonna keep trusting that I haven't done anything to deserve all this and just be supergood, and God's gonna make everything turn out."

She closed the Bible with a contented sigh. It was so good when you got everything all figured out.

When she went downstairs to help Mudda fix supper, Lily felt calm and halfway happy. Obviously Mudda's quiet time hadn't gone as well because she was scowling into the refrigerator when Lily got to the kitchen.

"I had a casserole all ready to put in the oven," she said. "Where has it disappeared to?"

*Probably sprouted legs and walked off,* Lily thought. But she caught herself. Job would never have thought that.

"Want me to look?" she said instead.

"To what end?" Mudda said.

"Huh?" Lily said.

Mudda closed her eyes.

"I mean, 'excuse me'?"

"If it were there, I'd see it. I'm not feeble yet."

Lily took in a try-again breath. "Mom always says two pairs of eyes are better than one when we're all looking for something."

"Lilianna, do stop chattering and get the silverware out. Someone has obviously absconded with my casserole, and I'm going to have to start over on dinner."

"Unless it was a pizza, Joe and Art didn't take it," Lily said.

"No, it was not a pizza," Mudda said. Her voice sounded tight. "I do not feed my family junk."

Lily bit her lip and counted out forks.

"Now remember that it isn't just about putting the knives on the right side," Mudda went on in that same taut voice. "Don't forget the condiments—your butter, salt, and pepper."

"I know," Lily said. In spite of Job, she heard her voice getting tight. How did the guy do it? This was hard.

She set the silverware on the table and opened the refrigerator. The margarine tub, of course, was all the way in the back. She sighed and lifted out the ketchup, a gallon of milk, and a CorningWare dish with a lid. She frowned at it.

"Mudda?" she said. "Is this your casserole?"

Mudda didn't turn around from the counter where she was chopping celery like it needed to be beaten into submission.

"The casserole is gone. I searched that entire refrigerator, which I am going to show you how to clean out tomorrow. It obviously hasn't been done in six months." She finally turned around. "Where did you get that?" she said.

"In here," Lily said.

"No, you did not. Now where was it?"

*What is it about "in the refrigerator" that you don't understand?* Lily thought. She could feel her face starting to go blotchy.

"Don't give me one of your silences, Lilianna," Mudda said. "Where was that casserole?"

"I *said* it was right in here. I moved the milk and the ketchup, and there it was."

"Don't take that tone with me, and do not under any circumstances prevaricate with me."

"How can I do that?" Lily said. She knew her face was bright red by now. "I don't even know what 'pre-whatever it is' *means!*"

"It means lie. It doesn't matter whether it is done in the context of a practical joke or not, it is still a lie. I won't have it."

Lily wanted to scream. Instead, she pulled her words together like a fist and let them fly. "What do you want me to say, that I came down here while you were having your quiet time and put the casserole behind the cookbooks where you couldn't find it and then pulled it out just now so you'd feel stupid?" So much for Job.

"I have told you not to use that sarcastic tone with me!" Mudda said.

"What difference does it make what tone I use?" Lily cried. She was close to tears by now. "You hate *all* my tones!"

"What in the world is going on in here?" It was Mom in the kitchen doorway.

"Your daughter and I are having a discussion," Mudda said.

"Discussion?" Mom said. Her mouth was twitching. "It sounded like the *Jerry Springer Show.*"

"I don't find it at all amusing, Joanna. We need to speak about Lilianna's attitude."

"There's nothing wrong with my attitude, Mom!" Lily said. "She just—I can't even—she's always—"

"Lil, why don't you go on up to your room and calm down."

"I want you to hear *my* side!" Lily said.

"And I will, now go."

"Hear mine first!"

"Lily. Go now!"

The twitches had disappeared, and Mom's eyes were stern.

"This is *so* unfair!" Lily cried as she flounced out of the kitchen with the tears already in her throat. "It's just *so* unfair!"

With his toenails skittering across the floor, Otto followed her up to her room. He was on the bed curled up with his paws over his eyes before she could even throw herself down and sob. When Dad came home, she heard a long exchange of murmuring voices in the kitchen below, and then finally, Mom and Dad came up the stairs. Otto gave a whine and dove under the bed.

"Where are you to growl at somebody when I need you?" Lily said.

Her parents' faces were grim as they came in. Lily stared down at her knees.

"Let's hear your side of the story," Dad said.

Lily was more than happy to pour it out for them. When she'd gotten it down to the last drop, she took a deep breath and waited. Surely they would see it her way and send Mudda packing back to Pennsylvania.

"This is a difficult situation, I'll grant you that," Dad said. "Your grandmother operates from a different paradigm than we do, and—"

"You'd better speak English, hon," Mom said.

Dad grinned. "Sorry. All right—Mudda has a different set of principles for living than we do. Actually, she has the same principles. She just has a different way of carrying them out. They aren't wrong—they're just different."

"What does that have to do with her calling me a liar?" Lily said.

"We've spoken to her about that," Dad said. "The point is—"

"Is she going to apologize to me?"

"That's up to her."

"Don't you think she should?"

"The point is that under no circumstances are you to use a disrespectful tone of voice with your grandmother," Dad said. "We all joke around here in our house, and at times I'll grant you it gets somewhat out of hand, but a surly, sullen, scornful tone is never appropriate. Am I clear?"

"Does she have to change her tone with *me?*" Lily said.

"That's up to her."

"How come—"

"Because you are our daughter and we are responsible for the way you behave," Dad said. "You, of course, do have a choice. You can elect not to follow this mandate."

"What happens then?" Lily said.

Mom and Dad exchanged one of those glances.

"No party," Mom said.

"*What?*" Lily said.

Otto poked his nose out from under the bed and growled. Dad looked down at him.

"You heard Mom," he said. "If Lily uses an uncivil tone of voice with her grandmother again, she won't be allowed to have her party."

"I don't think this is fair!" Lily said. "She called me a liar!"

"And I hate that for you," Mom said. "And I hope you two get that straightened out. But do it with respect or don't do it at all."

"You don't know what it's like here with her all day!" Lily said. "I feel like Job!"

"What?" Mom said.

"I know it isn't easy, Lilliputian," Dad said. "But keep trying. You two haven't even begun to get to know each other as women yet."

*And I don't* want *to!*

Her parents left then, each with a kiss on her forehead. When the door shut, Otto stood at it and barked, rear end up in the air, teeth bared.

"That's exactly what I wanted to say," Lily told him. And then she put her face into her pillow and cried.

Chapter
9

The next morning, when Lily was all cried out, it was clear that the only thing to do was be as polite to Mudda as she possibly could. She wished she could say it was because of Job—because of God—but it wasn't. With the party only two weeks away, it was time to send the invitations out, and once people knew about the party, it would be totally humiliating to cancel it. She'd have to move out of town or something.

So Lily dutifully cleaned out the refrigerator and wrote about *Pilgrim's Progress* in her journal and then spent her two non-Mudda hours blowing up balloons, coloring them to look like beach balls, putting the party information inside each one, and then letting the air out to put them into envelopes. It was the best thing she could think of under the circumstances. At least Adolf was behaving himself, so she could count on her ten dollars a week.

Mudda didn't apologize for accusing Lily of lying, and that made Lily break into a sweat on her upper lip every time she thought about it. Plus, Mudda kept right on criticizing Lily's every move until twice Lily had to run upstairs to her room with the excuse that she had to check on Otto, when what she really needed to do was scream into her pillow.

She went back to Job a couple of times, but what worked for him didn't seem to work for her. God was being very quiet, and Lily didn't appreciate that.

One thing did help though, something unexpected. The spotlight at the dinner table was turned on Art now, because Joe had let it out of the bag that Art had a girlfriend.

"Really?" Mom said that first night. She was out and out grinning over a forkful of chicken divan. "You're sweet on a girl?"

"I'm going out with somebody, yes," Art said, glaring at Joe.

"How come you didn't tell us?" Lily said.

He turned his glare on her. "Because I didn't want to be interrogated, like I'm being right now."

"Oh," Lily said, and she backed off. She knew what that was like.

"You're taking a young woman out, Arthur?" Mudda said. "I haven't seen you go out to pick anyone up for a date."

"We don't do that any more—my generation. We just kinda hang out in groups, only she and I are together."

"I like that better anyway," Mom said.

"And what does 'together' mean exactly?" Mudda said.

"Do I have to answer that?" Art said to Dad.

"Don't you want to know, Paul?" Mudda said. "I think those are the sorts of words a parent needs to have defined in this day and age."

"Never mind, Dad," Art said. "I got nothing to be ashamed of."

Mudda winced, and Lily knew she was dying over Art's grammar, but she waited intently. It was obvious to Lily that she really wanted that definition. Lily felt herself going blotchy *for* Art.

"It means we hold hands, hug, talk on the phone about us—and we don't do any of that with anybody else." Art gave Mudda a long look as if to say, *Is there anything else you want to know about my personal life?*

"When are we going to meet this young lady?" Mudda said.

Art shrugged. "I don't know."

"You should bring her to dinner so we can all get to know her."

"Why?" Art said. "We aren't engaged or anything."

"Wouldn't you bring any of your male friends home for your family to meet?"

"Not on purpose," Art said. "I mean, if they meet them, fine. If they don't, no big deal."

"We know all of Art's friends," Mom said. "Although I didn't know about—what's her name?"

"Bonnie," Joe said in a high-pitched voice.

He batted his eyelashes a couple of times until Art let him have it across the shoulder. Mudda looked at them both disapprovingly. Mom's mouth twitched.

"Bring Bonnie to dinner," Mudda said.

"Nah, that's okay," Art said. His entire neck was red now. Lily actually felt sorry for him. "We're both pretty busy."

"She's in band too?" Mom said.

"Yeah, plus she works at the animal shelter."

*Oh,* that *girl,* Lily said to herself.

"She still has to eat," Mudda said.

Art stabbed at a hunk of chicken with his fork. "Look, Mudda," he said, "I know you're trying to do the whole etiquette thing and all that, but I really don't want to bring Bonnie over here and have everybody give her the third degree over the spinach salad, okay? You'll meet her sometime."

"How about at my party?" Lily said. "She could come over and you guys could help with the games or something."

Art looked a little confused as his eyes darted from Lily to Mudda and back again. Finally, he said, "Sure. Yeah. That works. Look, could I be excused?"

"Got a hot date?" Joe said.

"Yeah, something like that." He punched Joe again. "Like you'd even know what a hot date was."

"I do," Joe said. "It's when—"

"Never mind, Joseph," Mom said. "You go ahead, Art."

"Where *are* you going, Arthur?" Mudda said.

"A bunch of us are getting together over at Ricky's to jam. Okay, Mom? Dad?"

"Just be in by curfew," Dad said.

When he'd disappeared from the kitchen, Mudda looked at them both as if they'd shot Art in the back or something.

"You allow this jamming?" she said.

"He's practicing his jazz with the other musicians," Mom said. "They call it jamming."

"You're certain it has nothing to do with the drug world?"

Joe opened his mouth as if to howl. Mom plastered her hand over it. Dad blinked behind his glasses and said, "Did I miss something?" Lily excused herself to go address invitations.

The day after they went out, the phone calls started to come in.

Reni said, "I asked Sigmund not to make any changes in my schedule because I have to go to your party or you'll never speak to me again."

"Don't you *want* to come?" Lily said.

"Sure. You're still doing the beach thing, huh?"

"Yes."

"Hmm, okay."

When Suzy called, she said politely, "My mother wants to know if I'm supposed to bring anything."

"Nope," Lily said. "Everything's taken care of."

Lily wished that were entirely true, but it would be by the time party day rolled around.

Suzy cleared her throat. "She also wants to know if there's going to be plenty of adult supervision around the pool."

"Of course!" Lily said indignantly. "Don't you want to know what kinds of games we're going to be playing and stuff?"

"No," Suzy said. And then she quickly added, "I'm sure it'll be fun." Her voice didn't sound sure at all.

Kresha, naturally, was all bubbly about it, so much so that she lapsed into Croatian. At least she sounded excited.

Lily had sent Zooey an invitation hoping when she saw the balloon, she'd change her mind about coming.

"Why did you send me this?" Zooey said when she called. "You know I'm not—"

"Oh, come on, Zooey. You have to come!" Lily said. "All the Girlz are going to be there. It isn't going to be right without you."

"Is it still a beach party?"

"Yeah, only it's not really the beach. There won't be any waves or sharks if that's what you're afraid of, and you're taking swimming lessons so you don't have to worry about drowning."

Zooey burst into tears again and hung up.

By the end of the week, all the girls on the list had called with an RSVP—they were all coming, even Ashley and Chelsea. That made Lily more determined than ever to make this the ultimate bash. She started making place cards for the table the minute Mrs. Woods paid her and she got to Wal-Mart for supplies. Each one was going to be a tiny sign with an arrow and *beach* on it that would have a toothpick post and a wad of clay to sit in. Each one would have the person's name on it.

"Ashley and those guys are going to be *so* impressed," she told Otto. She would have shared the thought with Reni and Suzy and the rest, but everybody was way too busy to yak on the phone anymore. However, when she realized that none of the boys on the invitation list had responded yet, she had to tell somebody. She found Mom in the laundry room with a book.

"Why are you reading in here?" Lily said.

Mom jumped a foot and tossed the book into a basket of folded underwear. "What's up, Lil?" she said.

Lily gave the book another quizzical glance but then went on to describe her problem.

"Doesn't surprise me," Mom said when Lily was done. "Boys that age don't know RSVP from MTV. Besides, I'm sure not a one of them has shown the invitation to his mother. Did you mention food on there?"

Lily nodded.

Mom patted her arm. "Then I wouldn't worry about it—they'll show."

"But what if they don't? What if I feel like a geek when I give a boy-girl party and no boys come?"

"You've already invited Art—nice touch, by the way, Lil."

"Mom!" Lily could feel herself turning pale. "I don't have to have *Joe* at my party, do I?"

"No, hon, don't have a coronary. We'll make other arrangements for Joe. Even *my* sense of humor isn't that sick."

Lily still didn't feel terribly comforted, and she called Kresha, who volunteered to bring her brothers. Lily quickly told her that wouldn't be necessary and decided to keep the boy problem to herself from now on. Still, if only she could talk to Reni.

As it turned out, Reni called her later that night.

"Sigmund says I'm doing so well, I get to be in his recital at the end of the summer!"

"Cool!" Lily said.

"I know. I've only been taking lessons four weeks, and I'm already out of the beginning books. And guess what else?"

"What?" Lily said.

"We get to wear a long dress for the performance. My mom's gonna take me to the mall on Saturday to buy one, and she said you could come help me pick it out."

So it was arranged, and Lily was excited. They could have been going to drop off garbage at the dump and Lily would have looked forward to it. She'd spent so much time at home lately, she felt like she was under house arrest.

They found a dress pretty quickly—long and soft blue with a high waistline. Lily thought Reni looked like a princess in it. Then Reni's mom let them walk alone to McDonald's at the other end of the mall while she did some boring shopping—for placemats or something.

They poked in front of every window, even the computer store, just to take it all in, and Lily helped Reni pick out some earrings at Claire's to match the dress. It was an almost perfect afternoon as they headed toward the Big Macs—that is, until Lily spotted *them.* She stopped and clamped a hand on Reni's arm.

"Shad Shifferdecker," Reni said. "Come on, let's hide in the sunglasses shop."

But before Lily could even get turned around, Shad had spotted her and was poking his buddies in the ribs. They sauntered toward Lily and Reni, jeans hanging down below the tops of their boxers.

"Gross me out five or six times," Reni whispered to Lily.

But as they approached, Lily had time to think things through. This would be a good time to find out if they were coming to her party. After all, they were some of the people she wanted to put in their places the most with the ultimate bash she was throwing.

"Let me do the talking," she whispered back to Reni.

"Gladly," Reni said.

Finally, the boys got to them and stood there with the ball caps they never took off pulled down over their eyes.

"What are *you* doing here?" Shad said, as if the mall belonged exclusively to him.

"Shopping," Lily said. "What else do you do at a mall?"

"Shoplift!" Daniel crowed.

Leo found that extremely funny.

"You buying something to wear to my party?" Lily said.

"What party?" Shad said.

"The one I'm having on the twenty-third, " Lily said with elaborate patience. "The backyard beach party. I sent you an invitation."

"Oh, yeah," Daniel said. "It was that stupid balloon thing. My little sister done that for her birthday party." He smirked at Leo.

"So are you coming?" Lily said to Shad.

"I don't know. I don't usually go to loser parties."

"Loser party?" Reni said. She bore down on Shad. "You're lucky she even invited you. This party is gonna be rad."

Lily tried not to look too surprised as she nodded.

"It's true," she said. "If you don't come, you're gonna miss the big surprise."

"What big surprise?" all three boys said at once.

"If I tell you, it won't be a surprise," Lily said. "Du-uh!"

"Oh, yeah, huh?" Leo said.

"You ain't got a big surprise," Shad said with his hard spit of a laugh. But then he added, "So when is it?"

"July 23rd," Lily said. "And you gotta wear beach clothes."

"I don't gotta do nothin'," Shad said. He jerked his head at the other two, and they resumed their strut down the mall. Shad looked back over his shoulder and said, "This big surprise better be good."

When they were gone, Reni looked at Lily. "What big surprise?" she said.

Lily swallowed hard. "I have no idea," she said.

## Chapter 10

$R$eni stared at Lily, eyes popping. "Then why *did* you tell them that?" she said.

"Because I want them to come. I want them to see that I can do something cool. You said yourself it was going to be rad!"

"I only said that to shut Shad up."

It was Lily's turn to stare. "You mean you really don't think it *is* going to be rad?"

"I don't know." Reni's dimples deepened. "You just keep talking about how great this is gonna be, and I haven't seen anything great yet. Not that I don't believe it'll *be* great—" Reni's voice trailed off.

*Now I know nobody understands,* Lily thought.

Lily had to admit that night as she crawled miserably into bed that it was not so bad having Otto crawl in there with her. His little side heaving in and out against her leg was kind of comforting.

But Otto couldn't solve the problem of the big surprise Lily had promised Shad and those guys. In fact, it seemed like nobody could. The next day, Saturday, she picked up the journal, skipped past the party plans that weren't working out anyway, and poured her heart out on the next blank page. It was almost done before she realized whom she was talking to.

*I think I really blew it this time. I told Shad Shifferdecker, of all people, that I had this big surprise planned for the party—and I don't—but I guess you know that and you're probably pretty disgusted with me by now. But you see, don't you, God, that I have to show these people that they aren't the only ones who can do stuff or are important? I need them to know what I can do—that this is what makes me special. I need me to know it too. Will you please help me?*

The door opened and Mudda sailed in with a stack of Lily's folded laundry.

*Don't bother knocking,* Lily thought. But she sat up straighter on her bed and tried to smile. If she wasn't nice to Mudda, there would be no need to worry about a big party surprise.

"I'm glad to see you doing something constructive with your time," Mudda said. She pulled open Lily's underwear drawer and began to put the panties in straight rows.

"I can put those away!" Lily said. She hoped her tone wasn't disrespectful, but yikes, those were her *underpants*.

"I thought if I got this organized, the next time you *did* put them away, you'd be a little neater." Mudda sniffed. "I suppose I'm dreaming."

*Why is it,* Lily thought, *I'm supposed to be respectful to her, but she can be as rude as she wants to me?*

"Is that your Bible study you're doing?" Mudda said as she started on the socks.

"I already did that today," Lily said. "I was just writing in my journal."

Mudda turned around to face Lily.

"You keep a journal?" she said.

"I do now."

"I have to say I'm pleasantly surprised," Mudda said as she closed the drawer and settled herself, uninvited, on the edge of Lily's bed. "That's an excellent habit. I've kept a journal all my life."

"Every single day?" Lily said.

"Since I was, well, just about your age."

Mudda looked up at Lily's ceiling light, and for a moment Lily was sure that was going to be the next object to be cleaned. But her grandmother got a long-ago look in her eyes as she settled her arms in a comfortable cross over her chest.

"I wrote all about meeting your grandfather," Mudda said, "and graduating from high school. Going off to college—I was so afraid—I thought nobody would like me—"

"Did they?" Lily said. Mudda's eyes sprang to hers before Lily realized what she'd said. "I didn't mean—"

Mudda waved her off with her hand. "I know you think I'm an old grouch. That's all right, I'm not here to win a popularity contest. But I could have won some back then. I had a fair number of friends."

"I'm sure you did!" Lily said quickly.

"For heaven sake, Lilianna, be sincere," Mudda said. She nodded toward the journal.

"I hope that if I am your topic today, you'll give me a fair shake for posterity."

"Huh—excuse me?" Lily said.

"If you're writing about me, I hope you'll give my side of the story, so that my great-grandchildren won't think I was a complete curmudgeon when they read it."

Lily skipped over the fact that she had no idea what a curmudgeon was and shook her head. "Nobody else is ever going to read this," she said. "It's very private."

Mudda actually laughed. "Then it *is* about me!"

"No!" Lily said. "It's about my party."

"Ah, the ubiquitous party plans."

Lily frowned. "What does 'ubiquitous' mean?"

"It means ever-present. We're always stumbling over it around here. It seems to be everywhere."

"Oh," Lily said.

"So, what is the problem with the party that you have turned to your journal for wisdom?" Mudda said.

To Lily's dismay, her grandmother was settling in on the bed and folding her hands on her lap as if she planned to stay a while.

"I've given my share of gala affairs, you know," Mudda said. "Perhaps I could be of some help."

"I don't think so," Lily said. "I mean—you're—"

"Need I remind you that you are patterning your party after an article in a 1970 magazine? I gave that same party myself—in 1970."

"Nuh-uh!" Lily said. "You made the sand castles and had the kiddie pool with the drinks in it and everything?"

"Down to the beach umbrellas in the soda cups. I outdid myself."

"Was it the ultimate?" Lily said.

"That's a good word. And yes it was. Though I don't think one person there appreciated how much work I put into it."

"Nuh-uh!" Lily said again. "They weren't impressed at *all?*"

"I don't think so," Mudda said. "In fact, I remember writing in my journal the next day that perhaps trying to impress people was the worst possible reason to give a party." She looked intently at Lily. "I'm going to give you a piece of advice."

*What a surprise,* Lily thought. But she waited expectantly anyway. Anything was bound to help at this point.

"My advice is this," Mudda said. "If you were giving this party for the right reason, things might be turning out a little better."

*On second thought,* Lily decided as Mudda excused herself and left the room, *there are some things that definitely don't help.*

She climbed out of bed and opened her drawer. She was certain all the underwear saluted.

The next day Lily had just finished washing the light fixture from her room when the doorbell rang. When Lily saw through the window that it was Zooey, she squealed.

"I haven't even seen you all summer!" Lily said. "Can you come in—can you stay? I think we've got cookies—and not the package kind like Oreos or something—my grandmother makes real, like your mom does—"

Zooey shook her head, and for the first time, Lily noticed that her eyes looked droopy.

"Are you sick or something?" Lily said.

"Why?" Zooey said. "Because I don't want a cookie? Why does everybody think all I care about is food?"

Zooey's plump little face crumpled, and she started to cry. It occurred to Lily that Zooey had cried every time she had talked to her since their sixth-grade graduation.

Lily pulled her into the house and made her sit on the sofa while she got her some Kleenex, a glass of lemonade, and, just in case, a chocolate-chip cookie. Zooey took the cookie first.

Lily sat down on the floor and watched while Zooey finished it off and calmed down. When she handed Lily the empty glass, Lily said, "What's wrong, Zooey? You've been sad a lot this summer."

"I'm having a terrible summer," Zooey said. "A *horrible* summer."

"I get the idea," Lily said. "But why? What's going on?"

Zooey looked at Lily with begging eyes. "Would you please not make your party a beach thing, Lily?" she said. "I feel so left out because everybody's coming and I'm not—but if it's *that* kind of party, I can't—"

Lily scooted up onto the couch beside her before she could burst into sobs again. There weren't that many Kleenexes in the house.

"I don't get it," Lily said. "What's wrong with a beach party?"

Zooey shook her head.

"Is it the pool?" Lily said. "You flunked swimming lessons?"

"No."

"Are you worried about the no swimming right after you eat rule? I mean, not that all you think about is food, but, I mean—"

"No, Lily!"

"Then what?"

"I'm too fat and everybody will make fun of me in my bathing suit—just like they did at swimming lessons!"

For an instant, Zooey looked relieved, the way a person does after she throws up. But then she started to cry harder than ever. Lily put her arms around her.

"Who said you were fat?" she said. "I'll tell them off! I'll sic Reni on them!"

But Zooey wouldn't be consoled. The more she talked about the way the boys at the community pool had called her Miss Piggy and Jabba the Hutt, the more the tears fell.

"I hate boys!" Zooey said. And then her face lit up, just a little. "What if you didn't have boys at the party, Lily? That would be better. Girls talk about me behind my back, but at least they don't say mean things right to my face."

Lily gnawed at her bottom lip. "I've already sent out the invitations," she said. "I can't un-invite the boys."

Zooey threw herself down on the couch, and Lily knew there was only one thing to do. She went to the phone. For once, everybody was home. She let each of the Girlz talk to Zooey.

"You could go on a crash exercise course," Suzy suggested to her timidly. "Some of the girls in my soccer camp did that."

"Who care vhat a buncha boys think, anyway?" Kresha said.

"Zooey," Reni said, "get a hobby or something and you'll quit thinking about it. I hardly ever think about being so short now that I'm studying the violin."

But the only thing that seemed to calm Zooey down was Otto, who, after surveying her from under his fluffy eyebrows for a while, crawled into her lap and went to sleep. She petted his iguana ridge and sighed and was able to go home dry-eyed. But she still told Lily she couldn't come to the party.

All through church the next day, Lily couldn't get Zooey out of her mind. During the sermon, while they were singing hymns, and even when Dad took the whole family to the Londonshire for the Sunday buffet, she chewed over what was happening.

*I'm making Zooey feel bad about herself,* she thought. *If she didn't feel like she had to wear a bathing suit—or if I told the boys not to come—she wouldn't have to feel bad.*

*But this means a lot to me. Maybe I could just have her come spend the night one night and we'll have a private party. Or the Girlz and her—just us the way it used to be—*

Suddenly, Lily felt her own eyes tearing up, and she reached for the napkin in her lap to wipe them off.

"The food's not *that* bad," Art said.

He was sitting beside her, talking in a low voice like he knew she wouldn't want anybody else to hear. Lily looked up at him in suspicion, but there was no evil twinkle in his eye.

"Hang in there," he said. "It gets worse when you turn thirteen, but then it gets better after that, and by the time you're my age, life's pretty cool again."

Later that afternoon when her mom came in to check Lily's progress on the Bible study, Lily said, "Why is Art being so nice to me lately?"

Mom's mouth did its twitchy thing as she flipped through Lily's workbook. "It's the girlfriend," she said. "He has to be nice to Bonnie or she'll dump him. He can't just turn 'nice' on and off or he knows he'll mess it up, so he's being nice to everybody." Mom's brown eyes were twinkling. "Love makes a person do strange things."

"I'm never falling in love," Lily said. "All boys have ever done for me is cause me grief."

"Don't base your opinion of all boys on your brothers."

"I'm talking about Shad Shifferdecker."

"Him either," Mom said. "I take it he hasn't RSVPd."

"He's coming. So are his friends."

Mom looked at her closely. "I thought that's what you wanted."

She went back to perusing Lily's workbook. Lily could feel her thoughts scratching around her mouth like they wanted to get out. She opened it and let them—all except the part about the surprise.

When she was through, Mom's lips didn't look like she was holding back a laugh. She seemed serious.

"You've prayed about this, I take it," she said.

"Yeah."

Mom nodded at the workbook. "You've done great on your Bible study—you definitely got into old Job. Are you applying it?"

"If you mean, have I done what Job did, yes, and it didn't work."

"Bummer," Mom said.

She was quiet for a minute, and then she said, "You're probably going to have a hissy fit when I say this, but just hear me out."

Lily nodded.

"I think you ought to ask Mudda about this."

"Mo-om!"

"I know she's difficult. You don't think it bugs the life out of me that she has rearranged every one of my kitchen cabinets and drawers since she's been here? I can't find a thing! Not to mention the fact that I have to go into the laundry room to have enough peace to read a novel."

"Why do you let her do it?"

Mom gave her a look, and Lily had to laugh.

"Okay, so that was a dumb question," Lily said.

"She has become something of an infuriating woman, I'll grant you that," Mom said, "but I've known her a long time and I know how wise she is. If you can get past all the orders and the criticism, you might be able to let her help you."

"Do I have to?" Lily said.

"Nope," Mom said. "It's your choice. What is that noise?"

Lily listened and let out a groan. "That's chewing," she said. "Otto's got something under the bed."

"I'm afraid to look," Mom said.

She lifted the dust ruffle and let out an "uh-oh." Lily scrambled down in time to see Otto take yet another bite out of the corner of her journal.

"You evil dog!" she said.

Otto considered that for a second with a cocked head, and then he went back to chomping. Lily snatched the book from him and pulled it out. All four corners were soggy and chewed.

"We can find another home for this animal if that would help," Mom said.

"No!" Lily said. "He's about the only friend I've got left!"

Mom's mouth did twitch then. "You always did have such a strong sense of the dramatic, Lil." She got up and sidestepped Otto's attempt to attack her shoelace. "Think about what I said about Mudda."

"Okay," Lily said. And when Mom was gone she did—for about ten seconds. She couldn't imagine explaining her Zooey problem to her grandmother, or any of the rest of it for that matter.

The next day she'd finished her chores and quiet time and was just getting back from the store where she'd walked to get some party favors—little sample bottles of sunscreen and cheapie sunglasses— with the money Mrs. Woods gave her. Oozing sweat, she dropped her shopping bag on the dining table and gasped for a drink. The phone rang. It was Marcie McCleary.

"Are you still having that party Saturday?" she said.

"Of course," Lily said. She could feel her eyes narrowing. "Why wouldn't I?"

"Because of Shad and them."

"Why?" Lily asked. "They're coming, at least they said they were Friday night."

"Oh, they're coming all right," Marcie said.

Lily could imagine Marcie's freckles standing on end with excitement. This was bound to be bad news.

"*And,*" Marcie went on, "they said you said you have a big surprise or something."

"Uh-huh," Lily said—slowly.

"Well, they told me Saturday when I saw them at the movies that they have a big surprise planned for *you* too. Only, Lily, I don't think it's a good surprise. In fact, I think it could mess up your whole party. You know how they are. If I was you, I'd cancel it."

*Well, I'm not you, am I?* Lily thought.

"So—what are you going to do?" Marcie said, obviously anxious for a verdict so she could spread it around.

"I'm going to have my party," Lily said. "Those boys and everybody else are going to see what a real party is. I'm not afraid of them."

"You better be," Marcie said and with a hurried good-bye hung up.

*This couldn't get any worse,* Lily thought.

And then it did.

"I hate to say I told you so," Mudda said from the doorway. "But I did. Now suppose you sit down here and listen to me."

Chapter 11

Lily sank miserably into a kitchen chair and groaned inside. *Here it comes,* she thought. *A whole lecture about what a moron I am.*

"I'm not going to pretend I didn't hear your end of that conversation," Mudda said, "and I just want to have my say about it." She straightened the placemats as she talked, her wiry hands pressing them like little irons. "You are giving this party for all the wrong reasons. You're trying to prove something—gain popularity—show them all how it's done. Isn't that true?"

"Well—yes," Lily said.

Mudda's eyebrows arched up. "At least you're honest. Now let me put this to you: Do you think anyone who is coming to a party to be shown up is going to have a good time?"

Lily hadn't thought about it that way. The minute she did consider it, she had to say no. It was just that it was so hard to admit that to somebody who was waiting to pounce with another "I told you so."

But as Lily nodded slowly, some of the wrinkles seemed to ease out of Mudda's face. "Now we're getting somewhere," she said.

Lily could feel the prickles of resentment on the back of her neck. "So—you think I should cancel the party. That's what Marcie said.

She said some of the boys are planning to play a trick on me that will ruin the whole thing." Lily scowled down at her fingernails. "You think I ought to, huh?"

"Absolutely not!" Mudda said. "Your friends are a bunch of ungrateful urchins who don't have the manners of raccoons. They *need* to be taught some socialization as far as I can see, but they can't know they're being taught. That's where changing your focus will come in."

"I don't think I even know what you're talking about," Lily said.

"Of course you don't. But if you're willing, I can help."

"You mean—with giving the party?" Lily said. She had visions of a punch bowl with fruit floating in it and boys being handed neckties at the door.

"Suit yourself," Mudda said. "But think it over first."

Lily didn't have to think it over, but she knew it wouldn't be a good idea to give Mudda a flat no.

"Thanks," Lily said. "I'll think—"

She stopped, mouth frozen, as her eyes went to the kitchen doorway. Otto was standing there, the remains of a pair of red plastic sunglasses hanging from his mouth.

"*Now* what has that beast destroyed?" Mudda said.

"My party favors!" Lily cried. She made a lunge for Otto, but when she grabbed him, he slithered through her grasp and under the table. He was covered with something greasy and damp.

"What on earth is that smell?" Mudda said. "When did I cook with coconut?"

"It's sunscreen," Lily said. Her voice sounded limp, even to her. "That was my other party favor."

Hardly daring to look, Lily went into the dining room. The bag was on the floor, and its contents were strewn in all directions and in various stages of chewed-up-ness. The house reeked of coconut oil.

That was the end of it. The decorations were gone. The invitations had been so much less than she'd wanted them to be. There wasn't money for all the cool food she wanted to serve or the way she wanted to serve it. And now there wouldn't even be any favors to hand out.

*Mudda's wrong,* she thought as she stuffed the trashed shades and sunblock bottles back into the bag. *I should just cancel the whole thing. It's going to be lame—and a lame party is worse than no party at all.*

She dumped the bag into the garbage can in the garage and dragged herself up to her room. Otto was right on her heels and tried to squeeze in the minute she opened the door, but she stopped him with her foot.

"You are *so* not coming in here," she said. "I wouldn't be in half as much of a mess if it weren't for you."

She slammed the door with him on the other side of it and flopped down on the bed, pulling China on top of her. After a brief silence, Otto gave a sharp, indignant bark.

"Yap all you want," Lily said to him. "You aren't coming in."

There was, of course, more argument from the other side of the door, accompanied by so much scratching Lily was surprised he didn't make a hole right through the wood. Finally, after a final plea of pathetic whines and whimpers, Otto was quiet.

Lily pulled her head out from under China, but she was relieved for only about fifteen seconds. The silence was harder to take, because now she had to think.

It wasn't, after all, really Otto's fault. Not all of it. Not the Zooey part. Otto hadn't decided on a beach theme and insisted that everybody wear a bathing suit. Otto hadn't invited every boy in the class. Otto hadn't made it so one of her best friends couldn't come. Nor had Otto promised some big party surprise.

Lily couldn't stand the thoughts anymore. She snatched up her Bible study book and journal. Maybe the next lesson would be about helping a chubby person.

She wasn't too far into the Book of Ruth, which wasn't even close to being about people with weight problems, when the whining and scratching started outside the door again. This time, it sounded like

Otto really would like to claw a hole through it. *That* would definitely start World War III.

"I'll let you in if you'll knock that off," she said as she padded to the door and opened it.

Otto sat out in the hall and whined.

"Well, come in," Lily said.

The dog's ears went down, and he let out a high-pitched yelp.

"Look, I'm sorry. I was stressing out, okay. It's not your fault. Now come on in. I'm not going to stand here and beg you."

She reached down to take hold of his collar and drag him into the room, but Otto skittered backwards nervously and barked again, that high-pitched yip she hadn't heard him use before.

"What is the *matter* with you?" Lily said.

Otto's ears lowered almost to his shoulders and he turned, tail going feverishly, toward the steps. He stopped on the second one down and looked back at her. His iguana ridge was standing straight up.

"Do you have to go potty?" she said. "Why couldn't you have just told Mudda? Why does it always have to be me?"

She grumbled all the way down the steps, following Otto, who acted as if he were leading her someplace terribly important.

"You must have to go bad," she said. "I'm surprised you didn't just pee in a corner."

He seemed so anxious, she went to the front door, which was closer than the back, and opened it. Otto stood his ground, whining, ears down nearly to his toenails.

"What! You can only use the backyard? When did you get so picky?"

With a sigh, Lily stomped toward the kitchen. Otto tore ahead of her, still crying as if something were after him. Only when she got there did Lily see why. Mudda was lying in the middle of the kitchen floor.

Otto ran to her and pawed at her arm. She didn't move. Her eyes were closed. Her mouth was open, and Lily could hear her gasping, like getting air was hard. Lily flung herself to the floor and pushed Otto aside.

"Mudda?" she said. She grabbed her hand. "Mudda—wake up!"

Her grandmother's palm was clammy, and so was her forehead where Lily touched it. Her face, half pressed against the linoleum, was pasty white.

Lily lunged for the phone, knocking over a stack of cookbooks on the counter as she fumbled for 911. She could barely talk when the person on the other end of the line started asking questions.

"Don't hang up," the lady said when Lily had answered them all. "We have an ambulance on the way, but you keep talking to me. Tell me if you see any changes in her at all."

The lady kept up a steady stream of chatter in Lily's ear, but Lily heard almost none of it. She knelt beside Mudda, the clammy hand between hers, murmuring, "Please, God. Please, God. Please—God!"

Mom, Dad, Art, and the paramedics all seemed to arrive at the same time. Only Joe wasn't there, which was fine with Lily because there was so much confusion, so much calling out of numbers and letters and long words, so many questions asked of Lily—the same ones over and over—that finally she sank her face into her hands and cried.

"Please, God," she said. "Don't let her die."

"I don't think he will, sweetheart," one of the paramedics said. "Look there, she's starting to pink up already."

Mudda's vanilla-white face didn't look at all pink to Lily as they carried her out to the ambulance, and it seemed even less so later when they let Lily tiptoe into the intensive care unit to see for herself that Mudda was, indeed, still alive.

She was awake too, but there were tubes going in and coming out of everywhere, and all around her machines chirped and beeped and zigzagged their green lights across their screens. If this wasn't dying, Lily didn't know what was.

"She's had a heart attack," Dad whispered at her elbow.

"Don't talk about me as if I'm not even here," Mudda said. "I have no intention of dying yet."

That one sentence seemed to wear her out, and she closed her eyes. Lily's own heart skipped several beats.

"Dad?" she said. "Is she?"

"Mom, you okay?" Dad said.

Mudda nodded. "Just exhausted. They won't let you rest in this hospital. It's like trying to sleep in a—"

They never found out what. She drifted off again.

"Does she have to have one of those pass-by things?" Lily said.

"Bypass surgery? They have to run more tests, but they think they can treat her with angioplasty and medication and rest. Lots of rest." Dad shook his head. "That isn't going to be easy. We're going to have to tie her down."

"I heard that," Mudda muttered.

Something like a laugh came out of Dad. Only after she looked up at him did Lily realize it was halfway a sob too. There were big tears shimmering in Dad's eyes.

*It* is *his mom, after all,* Lily thought. *Even if she* is *a grouch. I'd hate it if it were my mom.*

Her throat tightened, and her own eyes blurred.

"I think we both need a Kleenex," Dad whispered.

Lily decided not to go back and see Mudda the next day. The tubes and the beeping and Dad crying were all too much. She volunteered to stay home and make sure Otto didn't destroy the house. Art was still in bed, with orders to be on alert in case Mom called with a change in Mudda's condition.

"Otto's kind of our hero, isn't he?" Mom said before she left. "The doctor said the damage would have been a lot worse if we hadn't gotten her in there so fast. Good thing Otto let you know something was wrong."

"Yeah," Lily said. "I forgave him for everything else."

"That was big of you," Mom said.

Lily didn't add that there wasn't anything to forgive Otto for anyway. The party he'd ruined was for sure not going to happen now. After Mom and Dad left to drop Joe off at soccer practice and go on to the hospital, Lily got her party list out to start calling people. She finished sharing a bowl of Cheerios with Otto and was about to dial the first number when the phone rang. Art was out of bed and in the hall before Lily could even say hello.

"Everything okay?" he said, hair standing on end. "What's up?"

"Your grandmother wants to see you," Mom said to Lily. "Have Art bring you in."

"Is she dying?" Lily said.

Mom laughed. "No, Lil. They've moved her down to a regular room, and she's already running the nurses' station."

"You don't think she's gonna say this heart attack was my fault, do you?" Lily said to Art on the way to the hospital.

He glared at her across the front seat. Girlfriend or no girlfriend, he didn't do "nice" before he'd had a shower and a mocha, and he'd had neither.

"Why would she think a stupid thing like that?" he said.

"Because we had this, like, heavy talk just a little while before she—you know—"

"I doubt it," Art said, his voice like gravel. "If that caused heart attacks, you'd have been the one to have one."

"Me!"

"You've been all stressed out all summer like you're planning the Olympics. No wonder Otto latched onto you. You're just like him!" Art sniffed. "I'm way too laid back for him. I should've seen that coming."

"Maybe me being stressed out got her stressed out," Lily said.

"Save the guilt for something you can do something about. Take responsibility for world hunger or something. Mudda, in case you haven't caught on, is set in her ways. She ain't gonna change."

But Lily didn't give up on the idea that Mudda was going to let her have it with both barrels for making her have a heart attack. Her mouth was so dry it felt like cotton candy without the sugar by the time she and Art met Mom and Dad in the lounge on the fourth floor. Dad had a pamphlet in his hand that said *Living with Heart Disease.* Mom was looking a little dazed.

"What's the matter, Mom?" Art said.

"I—just had a talk with your grandmother."

"What happened? Did she take a punch at you?"

"No, quite the contrary. Lily, go on in, hon. She's waiting for you."

Lily's heart came right up into her throat. "Do I have to see her by myself?"

"She wants to see you alone," Dad said. "But stay just a few minutes."

*Don't worry,* Lily thought as she made her way down the shiny-floored hall. *I'm not gonna stay any longer than I* have *to.* She even considered making a break for the elevators, but she heard her name being called from the direction of the nurses' station.

"You must be Lily," somebody said.

"Yeah."

"Right this way." The nurse's sneakers squeaked on the floor as she led Lily around the corner. "She described you to a tee—right down to that beautiful mouth. You do have nice lips."

"She said that about me?' Lily said.

But there wasn't time for an answer. The nurse led the way into a sunny room, where Mudda was propped up in bed with only half of yesterday's tubes still attached and only one machine giving the occasional beep. Mudda's face looked drawn and tired, but all the wrinkles sprang to life when she saw Lily.

"Lilianna," she said. Her voice was crackly and weak sounding, which surprised Lily. The next few words surprised her even more.

"Come sit by me," Mudda said. "I want to apologize."

# Chapter 12

Mudda gave a soft chuckle. "Don't look so shocked," she said, "or you'll be the one having a heart attack."

Lily did have to sit down on the stiff-looking recliner that Mudda nodded to. She was feeling a little weak in the knee area.

"You don't have to apologize to *me* for anything," Lily said. "I'm the one who stressed *you* out."

"Don't be ridiculous, Lilianna. If I can't handle a twelve-year-old, it's my own fault. Besides, you're the most promising person in that house—and if you tell anyone I said that, I'll deny it."

Lily stared.

"Now, if you'll give me a chance, I want to set the record straight," Mudda was saying. "These doctors have informed me that I'm going to have a simple procedure to clear out one of my arteries. It isn't even surgery, that's how mundane it is. But I'm going to have to make some major lifestyle changes if I'm going to avoid an operation in the future. That includes, among other things, a slower, less stressful lifestyle."

Mudda chuckled again. "I told them the only thing stressing me out was being taken care of by a bunch of doctors who don't look old enough to be out of high school. But they said when they brought me in my veins were bulging while I was telling the paramedics how to handle the gurney—that was the kind of unnecessary stress they were talking about. The kind I create."

She wasn't chuckling anymore. Her eyes were cloudy.

"Maybe you shouldn't get so upset," Lily said, glancing nervously at the bleeps on the screen.

"The only thing that's going to upset me right now is if people start treating me like an invalid," Mudda said. "Now let me get this out."

"Okay," Lily said. But she kept her eyes on the screen. Mudda closed hers.

"I spent half the night talking to one of the nurses. Bright little thing. Graduated from the University of Pennsylvania nursing program—get to the point, Lilian."

Lily was about to protest that she hadn't said a thing, when she realized Mudda was talking to herself. Her hands fidgeted on the sheet, but the bleep stayed strong.

"She didn't let me pull any punches," Mudda said, "once I told her I wanted to sort through some of this stuff right away. She said I'm going to have to give up being a perfectionist—and all the baggage that goes with it. Now listen carefully, Lilianna, because I'm talking about you too."

"What baggage?" Lily said. "I didn't think I was carrying any."

"Not until I loaded you up with it."

Lily shook her head. "I'm so confused," she said.

"Here's the bottom line. I have to stop being so critical and negative and nitpicky. I have to let some things ride and start enjoying my life again. And I have to let other people enjoy theirs. I'm sorry, Lilianna."

Mudda stopped, and Lily saw her swallow hard. Her eyes were closed, but a tear slid down out of the corner of one. Lily got a Kleenex and wiped it off.

"Thank you," Mudda whispered. "I have just one thing to ask."

"Whatever you want me to clean, I'll do it while you're here," Lily said.

"No," Mudda said, "while I'm here, I want you to come in and talk to me. I want us to get to know each other as real people. That's all I ask."

Sneakers squeaked on the floor behind them. "Time's up," the nurse said.

Lily was almost disappointed. "I'll be back, Mudda," she said.

Mudda closed her eyes and smiled. All the wrinkles got soft.

That afternoon, after Lily had two more short visits with Mudda, Mom made her go home. When she and Art got there, Otto was scratching at the back door to get in. He'd already done away with the screen.

"Mom's gonna flip out when she sees that," Art said.

"I'll pay for it," Lily said as she gathered Otto up into her arms. He took a nip at her earlobe and nuzzled into her neck. She looked up to see Art staring at her.

"I thought you hated him," he said.

"No!" Lily said. "He's my dog!"

"I guess I came late to this party," Art said. He scratched at his head and left the kitchen.

It was the first time Lily had thought of the word *party* since that morning. Her heart sank a little, but she really was going to have to make those phone calls. Maybe she could do a back-to-school gig later when things calmed down.

She stood still for a minute, holding Otto, who was inserting his tongue all the way into her ear canal. *Wow, I thought I'd be hysterical if I had to give up my party, but I'm not even close. It's okay.*

She really did feel okay—until she made the first phone call, which was to Reni. She was home, and the minute she heard Lily's voice, she said, "What's wrong? You sound awful."

"My grandmother had a heart attack," Lily said. "She's in the hospital." And then she started to cry.

97

Fifteen minutes later, Reni's mom was there, fixing lunch for Lily, Art, and Reni, who she said could stay for the afternoon.

"I'll call Sigmund and cancel your lesson," she said. "This is more important."

Lily and Reni talked and talked and talked—about Reni's lessons and Lily's dog walking, about how hard it was to practice so much and how easy it was to resent your grandmother. Something struck Lily as they talked.

"We used to be exactly alike," she said to Reni. "But now we're so different."

"I don't care," Reni said. "I still like you better than anybody."

At least they agreed on one thing.

Art took Lily back to the hospital that night to see Mudda. She was eating some meat loaf that looked an awful lot like the food Lily had given Otto before she left the house.

"I'm going down to McDonald's and get you a Big Mac," Art said.

"That would be my certain demise," Mudda said. "But you *can* bug those nurses for a decent cup of tea."

Art seemed glad to be sent on an errand. Lily sat down in the recliner.

"I got to see Reni today," Lily said. "And we called Suzy and Kresha, and they're coming over tomorrow."

"And what about our friend with the bathing-suit phobia?" Mudda said.

"She wasn't home, but I'm going to call her later. She's gonna be really happy when I tell her I'm not having the party after all."

"*What?*" Mudda said. Her head came right up off the pillow.

"I have to cancel it," Lily said. "You're here—"

"I can see postponing it," Mudda said. "But cancel—certainly not!"

Lily glanced at the screen. Mudda stopped and chuckled.

"How am I doing?"

"You're stressing," Lily said.

"As well I should. Lilianna, you *must* have your party. I won't have you canceling on my account."

"It isn't just you," Lily said. "All the stuff's ruined, and let's face it, it wasn't ever going to turn out the way I had it in my head. It *sure* wasn't going to look like it did in the magazine—like yours did."

"And remember what I told you about mine. I think you should have your party, even if you do it a week later than you'd planned. My angioplasty is scheduled for tomorrow, and I'll be home the next day. And—" She looked right into Lily's eyes. "You would be doing it for the right reasons this time, so it's bound to be a success."

"I don't get it."

"You didn't see the look in your eyes just now when you were talking about your girlfriends coming over tomorrow. I haven't seen you look that happy all summer. That's what a party is about—friends getting together and enjoying each other's company. That's what you have that you can show to those ungrateful little urchins you've invited—what real hospitality is."

"I don't know if I know what it is myself," Lily said. "I just read that one magazine."

"You don't need a magazine. You are Lilianna Robbins. It's in your blood."

And then to Lily's utter amazement, Mudda winked at her. "Stick with me, kid," she said. "I'll show you how it's done."

"All right," Art said from the doorway where he was balancing a cup of hot tea and a handful of sweetener packets. "Who are you, and what have you done with my grandmother?"

The procedure went well the next day. When Mom called the house to tell her, Lily and the Girlz—all except for Zooey—danced around and squealed. Then Reni's mom made them ice-cream sundaes to celebrate with.

"Zooey would love this," Lily said. "I hate it without her." And then a light shone right into her thoughts like a flashlight beam.

"Hey!" she said. "Since I'm postponing the party, why don't I just change the whole theme so Zooey can come?"

"I thought you were all into the beach thing," Reni said.

"It isn't worth it if it's gonna make somebody not want to come," Lily said. "That's not a party—it's a performance."

"Wow," Suzy said. "How do you think up this stuff, Lily?"

"I don't," she said.

"Okay, so what's the new theme?" Reni said.

But Lily shook her head. "I think I wanna wait until Mudda gets home. I want her to help us."

All the Girlz helped make the phone calls, telling people that the party had been postponed a week. "Next Saturday," they told them.

There were, of course, a thousand questions.

Ashley Adamson said, "What if I have something else to do, Robbins?"

Marcie McCleary said, "Did Lily get grounded? Is that why she had to change it?"

Shad Shifferdecker said, "What about the big surprise thing? You still doin' that?"

Zooey said, "Is it still going to be a beach party?"

When Lily told her no, she broke out into squeals. Lily didn't stop smiling for the rest of the day.

Mudda came home the next day, looking less wrinkled and grouchy than she had—well, since Lily could even remember.

"Did she have plastic surgery or somethin'?" Joe said to Mom when Mudda was taking a nap.

"No, moron," Art said. "She's just getting more blood circulating. We oughta have some kind of procedure done on you so you'll get more to your head."

"Did you and Bonnie break up?" Lily said to Art.

"No. Why?"

Lily looked at Mom, whose mouth was about to twitch apart at the seams.

"No reason," Lily said.

Maybe even a girlfriend couldn't make you be nice to your little brother. Art was sure being decent to Lily though. He even said to her that afternoon when they went out to pick up Mudda's prescriptions for her, "Too bad you had to bump up your party. Maybe that little jerk Shad What's-His-Face won't come now. Did I tell you I saw him and his little sidekicks at the Acme the other day?"

"No," Lily said.

"They get to the checkout counter in front of me with about ten cans of whipped cream, like they're gonna buy it. The cashier gave 'em a hard time—wanted to know what they were gonna do with it. She was just kidding around with them, but they got all mouthy. Then— get this—she rings it up, and they don't have enough money. They go running out of there—almost knocked some old lady over."

"I bet they were buying that for my party," Lily said.

"You told them to bring whipped cream? What are you, crazy?"

"They told Marcie McCleary they were gonna play some trick on me at the party."

"Ten cans of whipped cream would've done it," Art said. He pulled Ruby Sue up to the front of Delk's Pharmacy and looked at her. "Are they coming to this party?"

"I think so."

"Dude, you're a glutton for punishment. But don't worry about it. I got them handled."

Lily stopped with her fingers on the door handle. "What are you gonna do?"

"I'm gonna make sure they don't trash your party. Don't worry about it."

It was getting stranger by the day. The better things seemed to be going for her new party, the less she felt she needed to have it.

Chapter
13

Mom said they couldn't talk about the party the first day Mudda was home. Just checking out of the hospital and getting settled on the couch in the family room, surrounded by pills, was enough stress for one day.

"I don't know if I'm going to be able to handle this slower lifestyle, Lilianna," Mudda said when Mom left the room.

"Don't worry about it," Lily said. "I got it handled."

The next morning, after Mom left for the school and Dad set up his day's work in his study at home, Mudda called Lily in and said they needed to get started. They had some decisions to make before any of the Girlz came over to help with the preparations.

"I need a new theme," Lily said, tapping her lips with the eraser end of a pencil.

"I don't know that you need so much a theme as a purpose," Mudda said. "What would you really like your friends to get out of this party?"

"You mean, like party favors?"

"Where is that magazine?" Mudda said. "I'm going to burn it. All right, let's approach it another way. Let's take your most difficult guest. Who didn't want to come to your party at all?"

"Zooey."

"How do you want Zooey to feel when she leaves this party?"

"Like she had a blast."

"Go on."

"Like she could be Zooey and nobody made fun of her."

"Precisely."

Mudda folded her hands as if they'd just completed an amendment to the Constitution.

"Precisely—what?" Lily said.

"Your purpose is to make every guest feel as if he or she can be exactly who he or she is without fear of ridicule. You want every guest to be allowed to be the person God made him or her to be. Only you don't tell *them* that, of course. They think they're just having a—what did you call it?"

"A blast." Lily sank her teeth into the eraser. "But how do I decorate?"

"What would your friends enjoy? How would they feel most comfortable?"

"They're all different!"

"Correct again."

Lily tossed the pencil aside so she wouldn't devour the whole thing. She'd been spending way too much time with Otto.

"So—I do something different for every guest?" she said.

"Well, perhaps *you* don't—"

Mudda's eyes gleamed. Slowly, Lily could feel hers starting to glow too.

"Are you thinking what I'm thinking?" Lily said.

Mudda nodded. "I always knew we thought alike," she said.

The next day, only Suzy and Kresha came over. Reni had a violin lesson, and Zooey had her last swimming class. Zooey told Lily on the phone she was so nervous about the test, she was sure she was going to throw up in the pool. Lily could hear her eating something even as they spoke.

"Zooey's back to normal," she told Otto when she hung up. He was pleased. He ran over to the cabinet under the sink and tried to get it open, so he could get into the garbage and celebrate.

Lily had everything ready for Suzy and Kresha when they got there. Kresha, of course, dove right in. Suzy didn't quite understand, but Mudda said she had to trust them. Then Suzy did whatever Mudda said. Heart attack or no heart attack, Mudda could still be pretty scary.

They made thirty plain invitations that said, "Don't dress for this party. Everything you'll need will be provided."

"They come naked?" Kresha said.

"Zooey *really* wouldn't like that," Suzy said.

"I like your sense of humor," Mudda told Suzy. After that, Suzy relaxed a little.

When the invitations had been dropped into the mailbox on the corner, they started in on their scavenging mission. They went through the boxes of clothes in the attic ("I knew I'd get somebody to clean that up before the summer was over," Mudda said) and the stuff Art said they could have of his, and then Mom drove them to the Goodwill store, where Lily spent some of the last of her dog-walking money on some outlandish touches. Dad carried one particularly cool old trunk down from the attic, and the Girlz stuffed it with their treasures.

"Play right now," Kresha said.

"Nope, we got more stuff to do," Lily said.

"She tough," Kresha said to Suzy.

Over the next several days, whichever of the Girlz who wasn't involved in camps and lessons and classes, came over to help. Even Zooey showed up—the day they made plain cupcakes.

"Why aren't we putting any frosting on them?" she said.

"We just aren't doing it *yet*," Lily said. "We're doing it at the party."

Zooey was still mystified, but she liked helping to get the toppings ready. She sampled some of each kind, but that was okay with Lily. It was good to have the real Zooey back.

"Did you pass your swimming test?" Reni asked her when they were all sitting in the family room with Mudda, going through a box of art leftovers Mom had gotten for them from the art teacher at the high school.

"Yes," Zooey said.

"Excellent," Mudda said. "Everyone should know how to swim."

"I don't know why I need to," Zooey said. "I'm never putting a bathing suit on again as long as I live."

Lily held her breath. She really didn't want to get Zooey all stirred up again just when they were having fun.

"Ladies, would you excuse Zooey and me?" Mudda said. "Why don't you go into the kitchen and fix us some tea?"

Zooey suddenly looked a little green, but Lily decided she had to trust Mudda.

"Is your grandmother going to yell at Zooey?" Suzy whispered when they got to the kitchen.

"No," Lily said. "I'm sure she's not."

"You know what?" Reni said as she handed a canister of tea bags to Lily.

"What?" Lily said.

"I think this is gonna be a rad party."

Lily grinned earlobe to earlobe. It was just one more reason she didn't even *need* a party anymore.

"But Lee-lee," Kresha said. "Do *he* got to come?"

She pointed toward the floor, where Otto was crouched down, rear in the air, growling at the lights that lit up in the soles of Kresha's shoes when she walked.

"Yeah, he does," Lily said. "I can't have a party without him."

When they got back to the family room with a pot of tea and a plate of Reni's mom's homemade cookies, Zooey didn't look as if she'd been yelled at. In fact, her eyes sparkled.

"You want a cookie, Zooey?" Suzy said as she passed the plate.

"Just one, thank you," Zooey said.

Then she smiled at Mudda, who smiled back.

For the rest of the week, until the next Saturday, the phone practically rang off the hook—and not just at Lily's house. Reni, Kresha, Suzy, and even Zooey got calls from people who had received their new invitations. Everybody had a question.

"What are we *doing* at this party, Johnson?" Ashley Adamson asked Reni.

"You'll find out when you get there," Reni said.

"Then I don't think I'll come. And Green won't either. And probably none of *my* friends. We don't do lame."

"I told her that was a bummer," Reni reported to the Girlz. "I said she'd be missing out."

"She'll be here," Mudda said. "That kind just wants you to beg her."

"Oh," they all said.

Marcie McCleary called *everybody,* except Lily, to ask them if they thought Lily was getting weird.

"What did you tell her?" Lily said.

"Trust your friends, Lilianna," Mudda said.

But Kresha piped up anyway: "I tell her *she* veird, Lee-lee."

Shad Shifferdecker called Lily and said, "This sounds lame, dude."

"Come see for yourself," she said.

"I might. I might not."

"What are people teaching their children these days about manners?" Mudda said when Lily told her. "Anything at all? But never mind—they can't all be Lilianna Robbins, can they?"

"Nope," Lily said happily.

But she was still nervous the day before the party. All the Girlz were there, and they were making sure they had everything covered. Even though the sign was ready for the front door, the clothes were carefully tucked into one trunk and the makings for decorations into another, the cupcakes were thawing and the toppings were in their little containers, Art had the CDs all organized, and Dad had picked up every kind of soda that had ever been canned—in spite of all of that, Lily was practically pacing the family room floor.

"All right, come here, all of you," Mudda said. "Sit down."

"Ve playing a game, Mud-dah?" Kresha said. "You teach us."

"Not a game, Kreshimira," she said. She'd seemed particularly pleased the day she'd found out Kresha's full name. Lily knew it drove her nuts that neither Reni nor Zooey had a "proper" name.

"No, Girlz," she said now, "I think we need to pray. After all, you're doing this ultimately for God."

There was only a short pause before the Girlz sat down around Mudda and held each other's hands. Suzy gave a nervous giggle, and Lily felt Zooey squirming a little beside her.

*Everything's awkward,* Lily said to herself, *when you first really learn how to do it—kind of like giving a party.*

After that, Lily was calm. She even wrote in her journal that night:
*Dear God,*
*I really am glad I'm having this kind of party instead of that backyard beach thing. Everybody can be themselves—especially Zooey. I don't care if I get popular because of this or anything. God, please just help people have a good time. Oh, and God, thanks for Mudda. She's not really that bad after all.*
*Love,*
*Lily*

Otto poked his head out from under the covers then and gave her a disgusted look.

"Okay," Lily said. "I'll turn out the light."

It didn't seem like 2:00 the next afternoon would ever get there. Even though the Girlz arrived at noon to do the last-minute things—

"Last-*minute?*" Art said. "They're two *hours* early!"—the time seemed to drag until the doorbell finally rang at 1:55.

It was Marcie McCleary. Her eyes were darting all over.

"I don't get this do-it-yourself thing," she said. "Are you sure it's gonna work? I bet it doesn't work."

"I bet you're wrong," Reni said. "Come on and sign in."

"Sign in? You don't sign in at a party."

"You sign in at this one," Reni said, and she showed her the big piece of white paper they'd put on the wall in the backyard. There was a bucketful of markers there.

"What do I write?" Marcie said.

"Write anything you want," Reni told her. "Draw pictures. Whatever."

Marcie stood there until the next guests arrived, trying to think of something. Watching her from the kitchen window, Mudda chuckled in Lily's direction. "This was an even better idea than I thought, Lilianna," she said.

Ashley Adamson came. And Chelsea. And all the rest of *her* friends.

*Huh*, Lily thought, *and we didn't even have to beg them.*

Once the boys began to arrive, it was obvious what had drawn Ashley's group. They flocked around the guys at the sign-in wall and giggled and shrieked and tossed their hair until Lily thought it would fly off.

"I take it that's the in crowd," Art said to her in a low voice as he dumped another bag of ice into the big tubful of sodas.

"Yeah," Lily said.

"That's who you're supposed to impress?"

Lily felt startled. "No," she said. "I don't think so."

She felt suddenly light and couldn't help smiling, at least until the last of the guests arrived: Shad Shifferdecker, Leo, and Daniel. Then a flock of butterflies gathered in her stomach.

It wasn't so much their just being there. There were plenty of boys gathered at the sign-in board, chugging down Mountain Dew and looking curiously at the big trunks on the patio.

No, it was the gleam in Shad's eye, the one that was reflected in Leo's and Daniel's, even from under those ball caps they never took off.

Marcie marched up to Lily, her own eyes darting with anticipation.

"They're up to something," she said. "I *told* you."

"Don't worry about it," Lily said. "We got it handled."

Still, she looked around for Art. He was right at her elbow. "This is gonna be so easy," he said. "I roughed 'em all up when they came in. They didn't know I was friskin' 'em. They're clean."

That made Lily feel better, and she told the Girlz they were going to stick to their plan. Everyone else stuck to it too. Mom was around, but she didn't hover. Lily was sure she had to be the coolest mother in New Jersey. Joe stayed up in his room, where he was supposed to be keeping Otto. The family had overruled Lily's opinion that Otto would be fine at the party.

"He snarls at anybody he doesn't know," Art had said. "Dad doesn't need a lawsuit from some kid who thinks he's getting his finger bit off."

"I couldn't have said it better myself," Dad had said. "Though I would have used 'bitten.'"

Right now Dad was nowhere to be seen, but Lily knew where he was. It was so fun to think of him being part of the big surprise that she had to stop herself from giggling out loud.

With everybody there, Lily stood up on the clothes trunk, and Art whistled really loud to get their attention. Out of the corner of her eye, Lily could see Ashley poking Chelsea and pointing to Art. She was tossing her hair.

*My brother?* Lily thought. *Oh, please.*

"Okay, guys," she said. "Everybody gets to make this party whatever's cool for you. First you gotta get dressed."

She pointed to the chest she was standing on. "There's every kind of clothes in life in here. You get to pick whatever you want—dress up however you want—so that you're the most *you*, you can be."

"And no fair doing what everybody else is doing," Reni piped up. "You gotta be yourself—that's the only rule."

"Do we get a prize for the best one?" Marcie said.

"No," Lily said. "Everybody gets a prize just for being here. That's part of the surprise."

"I want my prize to be her brother," Lily heard Ashley whisper to Chelsea. Lily was sure she was going to barf.

The minute she jumped off the trunk, the digging began. Lily circulated through the giggling, shouting, grabbing crowd and grinned as she watched them try on and discard and then light up with just the right thing. The only people who didn't play the game right were Shad and his buddies. They all dressed like girls, complete with balloons stuffed under their blouses. They left their hats on, of course.

"Interesting," Art said to them as they prissed around the patio. "You were supposed to dress like yourself. If that's how you see yourself, man—whoa."

The skirts came off seconds later.

Ashley found a pair of jeans of Joe's that were too small even for him and squeezed into them and strutted around wherever Art was. Chelsea and some of the other girls imitated her. Lily looked up at the kitchen window and saw Mudda shaking her head.

When everybody was fully outfitted, Lily opened the other trunk and told them to decorate according to their own tastes. She gave everybody a square yard of space to work with and let them go.

The result was a wonderful mishmash of color and shape and more-than-unusual décor. There was a mobile of styrofoam cups made into space ships, an entire zoo of balloon creatures, a shrine to the Backstreet Boys, and enough flowers made out of Kleenex to furnish a large funeral. Somehow Kresha managed to end up in the pool with her decorations, but Lily decided that must be her thing.

When Ashley wanted to decorate Art, and Leo made the world's largest collection of spitballs, Mudda nodded from the window and Lily moved the action on to the food.

"Everybody gets three cupcakes to put any toppings on you want to," she told them.

"Cupcakes?" Marcie said. "We used to eat cupcakes in fourth grade."

"With all the whipped cream you want on them?" Reni said. "And Skittles? And chocolate syrup?"

She went on listing things, but the noise of people trampling each other to get to the food table drowned her out.

Ashley and Chelsea decorated all of theirs with candy hearts for Art, and Lily wished she'd provided barf bags along with the napkins.

Shad tried to start a whipped-cream fight, but Art nipped it in the bud by finessing the can away from him and laying him out on his back on the grass.

But the rest of the cupcake creations were genuinely cool, ranging from a pretty good likeness of Larry Boy from Veggie Tales to a replica of a space shuttle. Some of the guys were really into outer space obviously.

It didn't take long to eat because most people wanted to save theirs instead of snacking on them. Lily moved on to the brainstorming for games. Everybody had to write down at least one game or activity they wanted to do, and Art pulled them one by one out of a paper bag. Lily thought Ashley was going to die when he pulled hers out. Mom nixed her suggestion that they play spin the bottle.

When Art drew Suzy's, she taught everybody how to do a round-off like she'd learned in gymnastics. Shad started to make fun of it. Then Art did one, and, of course, Ashley, and Shad was left standing on the sidelines.

When it was Reni's turn, she brought out her violin to play a couple of songs and they had to guess what they were. Ashley started to snicker. Art broke into applause, and they all clapped. He told Reni that musicians were cool.

"Are you a musician?" Ashley said to Art.

"Yeah," he said.

"Oh," Ashley said. Lily could almost hear her thinking about signing up for tuba lessons.

They played everything from charades to blindman's bluff. When Kresha tried to teach them a Croatian game, nobody could understand a thing she was saying, so they all fell into a huge, laughing pile. Then Mom came out with a surprise—the fixings for any kind of submarine sandwiches they wanted to make.

Lily's mouth fell open.

"My treat," Mom whispered to her as she went back to the kitchen for more mayo. "You deserve it."

Lily was too excited to eat. She just stood there, watching her classmates having the time of their lives, forgetting to impress each other, and being themselves. It was perfect. It was the ultimate.

She was turning to the window to catch Mudda's eye when something else caught hers. It was a blur of gray, streaking down from the back door and across the patio.

"Is that your *dog*, Lily?" somebody said.

"Well, it ain't her cat!" Daniel said.

Shad looked up from the two-foot-high sandwich he was building while seven people waited in line behind him. "That's the ugliest dog I ever seen," he said.

He set his plate on the table and crouched down. "Come 'ere, mutt," he said.

For once in his life, Otto did exactly what he was told. He bolted right for Shad, but he didn't stop when he got to him. Leaping up in a

113

wiry arc, Otto snatched up the bill of Shad's hat in his teeth and hit the ground running. Before anybody could even think about going after him, he disappeared into the bushes, hat and all.

"Hey!" Shad shouted. He plastered his hand over his head as if he hadn't felt his hair in months.

"Yeah, the hat's gone, dude," Art said.

But it didn't work this time. Shad's face darkened and, mouth hanging open in an ugly sag, he charged for the bushes.

"Give me my hat, ya little—"

Fortunately nobody heard the rest of it as Shad disappeared into the hydrangeas. All Lily heard when he backed out was Otto yelping in puppy pain.

Shad had his mangled hat by his own teeth and Otto by the leg, and Otto was protesting at the top of his bark.

"Stop it!" Lily cried. "You're hurting him!"

Shad flipped the hat onto his head and let go of Otto's leg, only to get a nastier grip on the back of his neck.

"You ruined my hat, ya stupid mutt!" he said, and he drew back his arm. If somebody didn't do something, his fist was going to land right in the middle of Otto's face.

Lily took the space in two leaps and yanked Otto out of Shad's hand. The fist flew into midair. There they stood—Shad with his chest heaving and his lower lip hanging to his Adam's apple, and Lily clutching Otto, now bravely snarling, and ready to snarl herself.

But when she looked up at the kitchen window, Mudda was there, slowly shaking her head.

*They can't all be Lilianna Robbins,* Lily could hear her thinking.

*I can hardly be Lilianna Robbins,* Lily thought.

But she took a deep breath. "You know what, Shad," she said. "If you don't have any better manners than that, I'm going to have to ask you to leave."

## Chapter
## 14

One of those really embarrassing hushes fell over the party. Nobody even whispered, not even Ashley and Chelsea. Otto was perfectly silent in Lily's arms.

Finally, Shad pulled his lip up from his chest and said, "No. I ain't leavin' 'til I seen this big surprise you say you got. Where is it?"

Lily couldn't speak for a minute. She wasn't sure Martha Stewart herself could pull this off.

But twenty-eight other people were waiting for her response. Not even Mom was coming to her rescue yet, or Art. When she glanced up at the kitchen window, Mudda was just nodding. All her wrinkles had sprung to life.

"Okay," Lily said. "If you promise to keep your hands off my dog, we'll show the surprise."

"If your dog promises to keep his teeth out of my hat!"

"Art, take Otto inside, would you?" Mom said.

Otto went willingly with Art, though not without a final growl in Shad's direction.

"Dude, that dog hates your guts," Leo said to Shad.

Shad told him to shut up, but nobody was listening. Their attention had been pulled to the hedge where Lily's dad was emerging—with a video camera in his hand.

"Were you in there this whole entire time?" Marcie said.

Dad smiled. "I was. I got it all on film."

"Do we get to watch it?" Daniel said.

Lily felt her face going into a grin again. "Of course," she said.

The Girlz helped her get everybody sitting on the patio with their sandwiches while Mom and Art brought out the TV and VCR. Shad and his buddies stood in the back—and Art stood close by.

The next forty-five minutes were the most hilarious of her life. There was so much shouting and laughing and covering of faces with embarrassed hands, Lily thought her own sides were going to split open. Even Ashley stopped tossing her hair and let herself laugh—except when she caught sight of Art rolling his eyes on video, at the back of her head.

The only person who never cracked a smile was Shad. He evidently didn't like seeing Art make him look like a party pooper when everybody else was doing gymnastics. He obviously didn't care for the way Art easily took him down on the lawn when he tried to start the whipped-cream fight. And he definitely hated the clip of Otto taking his hat and everybody else at the party enjoying it immensely. When they got to the end, where Lily told him he'd have to leave, Shad gave an elaborate yawn and said, "That was the surprise? Dude, that was lame and a half."

"Oh, Shad, it was not."

Lily stared. It was Ashley.

"I thought it was cool," she said. "Get a life, okay?"

Even Art laughed at that one. "All right, Ashley!" he said.

He went over to high-five her, and everyone else had to get into the act too. Only Lily looked back to see Shad's reaction. Only Lily saw him nod to Leo and Daniel.

"Art!" she shouted.

But it was too late.

Leo and Daniel both took off their ball caps, reached into them, and tossed something to Shad. He had already dug into the pocket of his too-big jeans and pulled out a book of matches.

"What *is* that?" Lily cried.

"Hey—no!" Art was running over a half-dozen twelve-year-olds to get to Shad, who was lighting something and smirking through his braces.

"No, man!" Art cried.

"What *is* it?" Lily shouted again.

"Stink bomb," Shad said pleasantly, and he hurled it straight into the group on the patio.

Girls screamed. Boys yelled. Sandwiches were tossed into the air and their contents dumped on various heads. The smoke added to the confusion, and with it, a smell more nauseating than anything Otto could produce in his pre-housebroken days.

In the midst of the chaos, Art wrestled Shad to the ground again and got the other stink bomb before he could throw it. While Art raced for the hose to drown it, Shad and his buddies vaulted the fence and took off, leaving Lily's ultimate party in ruins.

It was at least an hour before Dad and Mudda could get all the parents called, and Mom and Art got the girls and boys respectively out of their smelly costumes, hosed down, and back into their own clothes. Everybody waited in the front yard for their rides while Mom, Dad, and Art tried to fumigate the back. Needless to say, all the decorations had to be thrown away, and nobody was interested in sandwiches and cupcakes.

"Lily," Zooey said as they sat together on the front steps. "I think I'm gonna throw up."

And then she did, into the pot where Mudda had planted an azalea bush.

"At least she didn't barf on the walkway," Reni said.

That seemed to be the best thing anybody could say about the party. From the time the last person was picked up until two weeks later when they all went to Cedar Hills Middle School for seventh-grade orientation, the main topic of conversation was the stink bomb Shad Shifferdecker threw at Lily Robbins' party.

By the time Lily got home that afternoon, she was almost in tears. Mudda tried to calm her down with a cup of tea and some homemade snickerdoodles, but it all turned to soggy cardboard in her mouth.

"Nobody remembers the fun they had," Lily said, poking her index finger into the half-eaten cookie. "You'd think they all came in, sat down, Shad threw his bomb, and they went home. It's like nothing else even happened!"

"What *did* happen?" Mudda said. "What good things came out of your party? Think now, and stop feeling sorry for yourself."

Lily scowled, but she did think.

"Okay," she said finally. "Zooey didn't have to be left out. Except for upchucking, she had a really good time. She told me she didn't even think she looked fat in the video."

"That's worth the whole party, if you ask me," Mudda said. She'd gotten pretty attached to Zooey. "What else?"

Lily thought. "Ashley Adamson found out she can't have any boy she wants—at least, not *my* brother."

Mudda grinned, and Lily knew why. Right after the stink bomb went off, Bonnie had arrived, and Art had stopped hosing people down long enough to give her a big hug. Lily heard Ashley tell Chelsea she didn't think Art was that cute after all.

"But I think your Ashley had a good time," Mudda said. "At least, when she forgot herself."

"And she stood up for me against Shad."

"Who wouldn't? That poor unfortunate child is as close to unlovable as they get. What did his parents give him as punishment, anyway?"

"He only has a mom. She made him apologize to me on the phone. He was so fake, Mudda. It was disgusting. He was still bragging about it today."

"All right—tell me more good results."

Lily had to think hard. "Reni got to show them how good she plays the violin."

"How *well*. And yes, she does. I thoroughly enjoyed her recital."

Lily thought back to Reni in her long blue dress and her special earrings, making her violin sing in front of all the people at Sigmund's show a few nights before. Lily knew she'd been as proud as Reni's own parents.

"And Suzy too," Lily said. "She's so shy, she never shows anybody what she can do." Lily took another finger-stab at the leftover cookie. "Me—I show *too* much. Now everybody thinks I'm a moron for trying to have Shad Shifferdecker at a party."

"Think about what your friends showed *you* though, Lilianna," Mudda said. "I watched from this window, and I have to tell you, I was impressed. I didn't see any food throwing or bickering or insulting going on. You gave them an opportunity to be themselves, and people are always at their best when they're the most comfortable. You're a fine hostess."

"Me?" Lily said. "But what about Shad? He ruined everything."

"He couldn't ruin what your friends took home, trust me on that."

"Don't trust her on anything," Art said from the doorway. "She's an imposter. She hasn't yelled at me in a month. She can't be my grandmother."

A couple of days later, Mudda left to go to Maryland to spend the rest of her convalescence with Dad's brother and his wife, who didn't have any kids. She said with school starting soon, Lily's family was going to be busier than ever, and she didn't want to be in the way.

"In the way?" Mom said. "I'm going to be lost without you. These last few weeks have been great, Mudda."

Mudda sat Lily down in the family room while everybody else was loading stuff into her car so Dad could drive her to Maryland.

"Lilianna," she said, "I want you to promise me three things."

"Okay," Lily said.

"One—that you will continue to write in your journal daily. You'll never regret being able to see how you've grown."

"I promise," Lily said.

"Two—that you will keep talking to God, constantly, so you'll know who you really are in his eyes, not just who those little urchins you have to associate with tell you that you are. I'm not talking about the Girlz now. They're lovely young women. Stick with them."

Lily just nodded. She could feel the tears in her throat.

"And three—that the next time you want to give a party, you will consult me on the planning."

This time, Lily shook her head. "My Martha Stewart days are over, Mudda," she said.

"Oh, but your Lily days, I suspect, are just beginning." Mudda let her wrinkles soften for a second before she dug into her handbag and pulled out a small box, which she pressed into Lily's hand.

"Open it when I'm gone," she said. "I'm too old for crying."

Lily wasn't too old. She sobbed when Dad pulled the car out of the driveway, and she must have looked so forlorn that even Joe didn't give her a hard time about blubbering.

"I don't get what the big deal is," she heard him say to Art.

"No more snickerdoodles, dude," Art said.

"Oh, man!"

As they went into the house, Art patted Lily on the shoulder. That made her cry even more.

*I sure hope he keeps that girlfriend,* she thought. *I like him now.*

Then she cried again. But when she finally remembered to open the box Mudda had put into her hand, she stopped. No tears could express the feeling she had when she saw what was inside.

It was the daintiest of crosses, shining gold on a chain so fine Lily was afraid to touch it. But she did touch what was on the cross, mounted in gold, engraved by angels, she decided, and painted white and green with their holy brushes.

It was a lily. It sparkled in the sun when Lily lifted the cross out to dangle it from her fingers. That's when she noticed there was a note under it.

*I told you once,* Mudda had written in her perfectly curved handwriting, *that I wanted you to be worthy of the Lily name. Little did I know that you already were, but I know it now, and I want you to have this to remind you. Wear it in faith. —Mudda*

Lily's fingers shook as she fastened the chain at the back of her neck. Otto jumped up, his paws on her thighs. His tail was wagging at light-speed.

"This is the most special thing I ever got," she told him.

He barked, but she knew he didn't get it. She scooped him up into one arm and went inside to call the Girlz. She still couldn't tell them—or anybody—exactly who she was. But for now at least, it was enough just to be Lily.

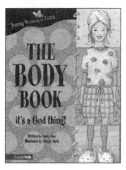
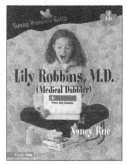

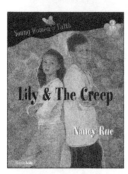

# NIV Young Women of Faith Bible

## GENERAL EDITOR SUSIE SHELLENBERGER

Designed just for girls ages 8-12, the *NIV Young Women of Faith Bible* not only has a trendy, cool look, it's packed with fun to read in-text features that spark interest, provide insight, highlight key foundational portions of Scripture, and more. Discover how to apply God's word to your everyday life with the *NIV Young Women of Faith Bible.*

Hardcover 0-310-91394-2
Softcover 0-310-70278-X

*Available soon at your local bookstore!*

**Zonderkidz**™

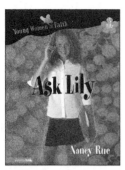
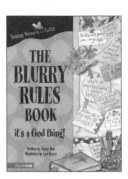

We want to hear from you. Please send your comments about this book to us in care of the address below. Thank you.

**Zonderkidz**™

*Grand Rapids, MI 49530*
www.zonderkidz.com